"Well, well...this is a nice surprise."

Priscilla couldn't believe it! "What are you doing here?"

"Ah, you'll have to forgive me for not recognizing you..." Dean's voice trailed off as he took a step closer, his impossibly wide shoulders pushing open the door fully, his gaze immediately darting around the floor of the room. "You look a little different without your sunglasses."

His perusal stopped the moment it landed on her bare toes, and his smile deepened as he slowly took his time letting his gaze travel up her legs. By the time he reached the edge of the towel that rode high on her thighs, a warm flush had enveloped Priscilla.

She should be annoyed at his deliberate scrutiny, but for some reason she was—pleased?

No, that couldn't be right. Just because her ex had rarely taken his nose out of his financial journals, even during a conversation, didn't mean she thought—that she felt—

"Or without your wet clothes," he added.

* * *

Welcome to Destiny:
Where fate leads to falling in love

Dear Reader,

A small ranching town in Wyoming is the last place Dean "Zip" Zippenella, a born-and-bred Jersey Shore boy, thought he'd settle down, but when his best friend needed his help, Dean moved west, and he now considers Destiny his home. He also considers himself pretty happy with his life, even if his dog, Daisy, keeps messing things up with the ladies. It's a bit tough to find a special someone to spend time with when man's best friend doesn't like females. Which of course doesn't explain why Daisy is so enamored with a socialite who's only in town long enough to pull together—wait for it—a bachelor auction! And yeah, somehow Dean has gotten roped into helping with the fund-raiser! Now if he could just figure out a way to help without losing his heart...

As a member of one of the richest families in the country, Priscilla Lennox has used the family name to quietly raise millions for charity over the years despite the press's exaggerated portayal of her lifestyle. When Priscilla suffers a heartbreaking moment, she decides she's had enough and leaves town ahead of the paparazzi mess sure to follow. She never planned to stay in the small town of Destiny longer than a few days, but the next thing she knows she's agreed to pull together a fund-raiser for a friend's summer camp. And that means working closely with the last man in the world she should be attracted to. But she is, and now Priscilla is wondering where exactly her home should be.

Dean and Priscilla believe they are very different from each other, but in truth, both are a bit on the outside looking in.... Hope you enjoy finding out what happens as they find themselves looking at each other in a new light!

Happy reading!

Christyne

Destiny's Last Bachelor?

Christyne Butler

ISBN-13: 978-0-373-65818-3

DESTINY'S LAST BACHELOR?

This edition published by arrangement with Harlequin Books S.A.

For questions and comments about the quality of this book, please contact us at CustomerService@Harlequin.com.

Printed in U.S.A.

Books by Christyne Butler

Harlequin Special Edition

^*Fortune's Secret Baby* #2114
Welcome Home, Bobby Winslow #2145
Having Adam's Baby #2182
¤*Puppy Love in Thunder Canyon* #2203
§*The Maverick's Summer Love* #2275
Flirting with Destiny #2289
Destiny's Last Bachelor? #2336

Silhouette Special Edition

The Cowboy's Second Chance #1980
The Sheriff's Secret Wife #2022
A Daddy for Jacoby #2089

Harlequin Books

Special Edition Bonus Story: The Anniversary Party—Chapter Four

^The Fortunes of Texas: Lost...and Found
*Welcome to Destiny
¤Montana Mavericks: Back in the Saddle
§Montana Mavericks: Rust Creek Cowboys

Other titles by this author available in ebook format.

CHRISTYNE BUTLER

fell in love with romance novels while serving in the United States Navy and started writing her own stories six years ago. She considers selling to Harlequin Special Edition a dream come true and enjoys writing contemporary romances full of life, love, a hint of laughter and perhaps a dash of danger, too. And there has to be a happily-ever-after or she's just not satisfied.

She lives with her family in central Massachusetts and loves to hear from her readers at chris@christynebutler.com. Or visit her website, www.christynebutler.com.

To the Bartlett Bunnies
Thank you for sharing your wonderful friendships
and asking a lot of “what if…” and “or maybe…”
questions as we plotted our books!

Chapter One

"You know that old saying 'Keep your friends close and your enemies closer'? Well, I think there should be another line." Priscilla Lennox had to raise her voice to be heard as she spoke into the tiny headset that permitted her to keep her hands on the wheel and off her cell phone. Added bonus? Not having to put the top up on her Mercedes convertible. "Keep at least a thousand miles between you and your family."

"Well, don't hold back, honey. Tell me how you really feel." Lisa's sweet voice still held that down-home Savannah-born-and-bred charm despite her years in Southern California. "Not that you need to explain this latest escapade of Jacqueline's, bless her heart."

No, Priscilla didn't need to bother with the details. Her best friend had heard often enough about the mishaps and misadventures of Priscilla's younger sister over the years. Not to mention how Priscilla had always wound up either being blamed for her sister's messes or cleaning them up before the press got wind of them.

Or heaven forbid, their father.

"I'm guessing you haven't seen the headline in the *Entertainment World* that came out today," her friend added.

Priscilla waited for a moment before answering. She'd purposely avoided the press coverage as she made her way through Northern California, into Nevada and now zoomed down the highway just east of Salt Lake City. Was that enough time—and distance—to prepare for the craziness headed her way?

"No, go ahead and read it to me." She hoped her words sounded causal as she released her tight grip on the steering wheel and flexed her fingers. Her hand was noticeably lighter now that the diamond she'd worn for the past six months was tucked away with the rest of her jewelry. Her *right* hand. "I'm braced and ready."

"'Commodities Millionaire Trades Good Deeds Sister for Good Times Sister.'"

Okay, the kick to Priscilla's heart smarted for a moment, but then it faded to a dull ache. Shouldn't she be more devastated by the clever turn of words? Maybe she was still in shock? After all, it wasn't every day that a girl walked in on her boyfriend and her sister in a clinch so sizzling they could've been modeling for the cover of a romance novel—the kind sporting a half-naked man and a lady whose dress was undone all the way down to her perfect backside. Yeah, that was one mess Priscilla most definitely hadn't stuck around to clean up.

"There's a montage of photos, too. You with Jonathan on his yacht last summer, Jonathan and Jacqueline arm and arm on the red carpet at the gala a few nights ago, you backstage that same night—looking marvelous in a Lisa Ashland Original, I'll shamelessly add—wielding that famous clipboard of yours."

Great. Her father would be so pleased to see both of his

girls in full color in one of the most popular gossip rags in the country, and probably spilling over to its website and nightly television show, as well. And he'd blame her, of course.

Sweet Jacqueline could never be at fault. No, not his baby. Not the sweet blessing that had arrived long after he and her mother had considered their family complete with just one daughter.

Priscilla sighed. It still amazed her that she was a week away from turning thirty and her life was still divided into two sections. The eight years before her sister was born and the twenty-two years since.

"So why are you heading for Wyoming?" Lisa's voice broke into her thoughts. "There's nothing there but…a lot of Wyoming."

Thankful for the switch in subject, Priscilla latched on to her friend's question. "Remember when I mentioned last week how I've been chatting with Bobby Winslow—"

"The retired race-car driver? What does he have to do with this sudden road trip of yours?"

"Well, Bobby started this children's summer camp in his hometown of Destiny, Wyoming."

"And he's asked you for help?"

"Well, no." A small detail Priscilla had never let get in her way before. "But we have spoken about fund-raising and promotion for the place."

Okay, so maybe Bobby had been joking when he said he should hire her. And maybe she'd been doing the same when she said she would send him an email with a financial prospectus. Even so, she'd started the research necessary for such a project just a few days ago.

Before her life had been turned upside down. Before she had nothing but time on her hands.

"I know this is going to sound rather snobbish, but isn't that a little outside of your area of expertise?" Lisa asked.

That was exactly why Priscilla had pointed her convertible to this part of the country after she'd escaped L.A. two days ago. "I'll admit a summer camp is less high-profile than organizations I've worked with in the past, but I've been looking for something new. Something different. I'd already planned to take the rest of the summer off to rethink my career options. The foundation means the world to me, but after ten years…" Priscilla's voice faded for a moment as she swallowed the lump in her throat. "Maybe I've given back enough."

"Okay, I get why you've abandoned your plans for a getaway to the French Riviera with the jerk whose name we won't ever mention again, but traveling solo through the Wild West instead?"

Solo? Priscilla looked over at the passenger seat, where her passenger snoozed away in a monogrammed sleeping bag on top of a tufted, lamb's wool pillow. "Who said I was alone?"

"Oh, please don't tell me you have Jacqueline's ugly mutt—"

"Sebastian Niles A King's Elegance is not ugly and he's not a mutt. He's a purebred smooth-coat Chihuahua my sister thought would make a cute fashion accessory before she realized a live animal requires actual care and feeding. And…love. Besides, I think the poor thing was as traumatized as I was by what we witnessed in that dressing room."

"Su-gar," Lisa drawled again, "are you sure about this?"

"About needing to get away from the craziness going on back home? Absolutely." An odd thrill raced through her at the thought of having so much free time ahead of her. Yesterday the country had celebrated its independence. Now it was time for her to do the same. "I'll visit Bobby and his wife for a few days, share some ideas I've worked up, and then who knows where I'll head next. Maybe Chicago or New York. Or a deserted tropical island with no media access."

"Well, wherever you end up, please remember to check in. I'll be up to my false eyelashes finalizing samples for next spring's collection, but that doesn't mean I'm not here to listen to your wild adventures."

Priscilla snorted. "I think you've got the wrong sister."

"Oh, no, *I* think you're destined for something wild. And wicked. You need to let down your hair and have some fun. And I mean that literally."

Priscilla automatically brought her hand up to the tightly wound roll at the back of her head. "I don't have the top up. The wind will make it a mess."

"That's the point of having a convertible. Don't tell me you can't remove a simple hair clip."

Of course she could. Priscilla had been wearing her hair in a Fresh twist style for so long she could put it up, and take it down, in her sleep. It'd been a style her mother favored, which meant Priscilla had always rebelled against it.

Until she wore it for the funeral. And every day since, it seemed. No, that couldn't be right. Her mother had been gone for fourteen years. Okay, so maybe she'd wore her hair this way ever since she started working at the foundation her junior year in college.

After a flip of her wrist, the warm summer wind took hold of her long locks, lifting and brushing them back from her face and neck. A quick glance in her review mirror revealed how different she looked.

"Feels pretty good, doesn't it?"

Priscilla had to admit her friend was right. "How did you know I did it?"

"I heard you sigh."

"It's just hair, Lisa."

"It's a start. Next up? Something wild and wicked. Just you wait and see."

The conviction in her friend's words brought forth a genuine laugh this time before she thanked Lisa for being so wonderful and ended the call.

By five o'clock that afternoon, Priscilla was exhausted. She had a cramp in her foot and her backside felt as if it was stuck to the leather seat beneath her. Plus, her sidekick was wide-awake and doing enough butt wiggling that it could only mean one thing.

Her car's navigation system told her the center of Destiny was still twenty miles away. Thanks to an internet search on her phone, she'd booked a room at a local inn, but her four-legged friend didn't look as if he could wait until they arrived to take care of business. After passing an impressive compound of log homes, she spotted a side road that led to a wide area near the river they'd just crossed. She drove there and pulled to a stop in the shade from a cluster of trees, shut down the engine and got out of the car.

"Don't get lost," she called out, peeling off her suit jacket as the pup headed straight for the woods. "This isn't like the manicured lawns of Beverly Hills."

Making her way to the water's edge was a bit tricky in her three-inch heels, but as soon as she found an oversize rock to sit on, Priscilla slipped out of her shoes and dipped her aching toes in the crystal blue waters. "I need to wear flats the next time I plan an escape."

Unable to resist, she stood and waded in farther, pleased to find the creek's bottom wasn't as rocky or muddy as she'd thought it would be. She looked around, noticing a rope hanging from a tree that arched over the water. The clearing was obviously well used. It was easy to picture a group of kids or a family enjoying a picnic here, but at the moment it was only her. With the cold water swishing past her calves and a light breeze caressing her bare arms, Priscilla reveled in the solitude of the natural surroundings, feeling as if she'd drawn her first deep breath in months.

No ringing phones, no disapproving fathers or whiny excuses from her sister, no annoying clicking and flashing from the paparazzi's cameras…

Just peace and quiet.

"Honey, I'm a man who needs female companionship."

Dean Zippenella hoped he sounded sincere, but a part of him knew he'd already lost this argument. Usually he had no problem when it came to charming the ladies, but this one—his favorite one—was stubbornly quiet in the passenger seat of his truck.

"Look, you've made your feelings perfectly clear, over and over again, and while I love our alone time, I'd like to bring a friend to the house once in a while without worrying you're going to do something crazy."

He tried to catch her gaze, but a quick turn of the head revealed that she was staring out the half-open window.

"You know, it's more than just your unpleasant attitude. It's your very unladylike behavior that gets you in the most trouble."

That got him a tilt of her nose that looked almost regal.

"Do I need to list them for you?" Dean kept one hand on the steering wheel and used the other to tick off the all-too-familiar offenses. "Peeing on their clothes, hiding their shoes, chewing on whatever you can scrounge out of their purses, including feminine products that no man should ever see."

Daisy turned to face him, offered a quick bark, and darn if the corners of her mouth didn't turn up into a cocky grin. Then he remembered the latest mischief. "And yes, that includes the cash you always manage to get out of their wallets."

His last guest had shrieked when she spotted the contents of her purse scattered at the dog's feet and the mangled remains of a twenty-dollar bill hanging from Daisy's mouth. Dean could've sworn the mischievous furball had been grinning then, as well.

That had been, what, almost two months ago? He'd tried to pay back the twenty dollars but the woman took offense. As if he'd been offering to pay for the time they'd enjoyed together or something. He'd been a lonely man after that. Something that hadn't happened much since he'd moved to Destiny, Wyoming, a few years ago.

The ladies liked him—or they used to—and he'd never been at a loss for company. As long as he spent time at their places. Once they got an invite back to his home and met Daisy, they quickly discovered Daisy had no qualms about showing just how she felt about human females.

She didn't like them. Any of them. Not even the women who meant the most to him. His grandmother, mother and three sisters, who'd all tried to win Daisy's affections when Dean had shown up at the family home in New Jersey, his duffel bag in one hand and a puppy in the other, after a stint in the army.

While the scraggly mutt he'd saved from a harrowing life in the Middle East had been devoted to him over the years and was friendly with any males she came across, she never changed her mind about the ladies.

Deciding to end this one-sided discussion, Dean checked his watch, noting he had at least an hour before his last physical-therapy patient of the week. He'd finished his shift at the veterans' center in Cheyenne earlier than planned and returned home to pick up Daisy. She always accompanied him whenever he worked with his favorite patient and then they'd grab some takeout for dinner.

After that, the evening, and the rest of the weekend, stretched out in front of him.

Rounding the bend in the road, Dean spotted a red convertible parked down by the river. He frowned. Not the typical style of car found around Destiny, where pickup trucks like his were the favorite mode of transportation.

He wondered if someone might be in trouble. Turning down the dirt road, he pulled to a stop on the far side of the clearing. The sight of a beautiful blonde bombshell cooling off in the Blue Creek River caught him by surprise.

Bellissima! *Where in the world did you come from?*

He tossed his sunglasses up on the truck's dashboard while pressing a button, raising both the windows. "Sorry, sweetheart. I know you love to play in the water, but someone else got here ahead of you," he said to Daisy.

He exited his truck, but left the engine and the air-conditioning running, and headed for the riverbank. His steps slowed as he enjoyed the view of the stranger's sexy legs when she lifted her skirt high on her thighs as she waded into deeper water. From the fancy suitcases piled in the backseat of her car to the clothes she wore, it was easy to see this beauty definitely wasn't from around here. In fact, she seemed more big-city chic than country simplicity—

Suddenly a blur of golden-brown raced past him.

"What the hell?" Dean had no idea how Daisy had managed to roll down the window enough to squeeze out, but she was making a beeline for the water's edge.

And for the unsuspecting lady.

"Daisy!" Oh, man, this had trouble written all over it. "Daisy, get back here!"

His dog wasn't listening. Nope, she headed straight for the water nymph.

The woman had spun around when he yelled. Blond waves flowed over her shoulders and dark sunglasses shaded her eyes. Her luscious mouth dropped open in surprise at the sight of him and his dog.

She stumbled back a few steps the moment Daisy charged in, splashing her way right to the woman before suddenly halting in front of her.

And damn if Daisy's tail didn't start wagging just above the waterline.

The woman started to smile and then leaned down, one hand outstretched toward his pet. A typical reaction, but Daisy wasn't a typical dog.

Dean called out, "Stop! Don't touch her."

The nymph froze in place for a moment before slowly straightening, her free hand retreating to her chest. She was probably unaware she still held the ends of her skirt hiked up way past her knees with the other.

She stared at him—at least Dean thought she did behind those dark sunglasses—before she looked down at Daisy. Then she directed her gaze back to him, her chin lifting a bit. "I was only going to say hello."

Her voice was as smooth and silky as the finest Chardonnay. Dean stopped when his boots hit the water's edge, sinking a bit into the soft earth. "That's probably not a good idea. She can be...unpredictable. Daisy, come here, girl."

Daisy ignored him, keeping her gaze on the blonde, who glanced at the dog again before looking at Dean. "Does she bite?"

She never had, but he hated to think there might be a first time.

"No. I don't think so." He'd found Daisy in the desert during his last tour in the Middle East. The thirty-pound, two-foot-tall mutt resembled a Portuguese Podengo. Granted, she wasn't growling and her wirehaired fur wasn't bristling, but who knew what went on in a female's mind—canine or human.

The woman took another step backward. "Well, she's the one who came to me. Up until a moment ago I was enjoying a few minutes of blessed solitude."

Hmm, a hint of snobbishness. "Yeah, well, she can be somewhat unfriendly at times."

"The wagging tail notwithstanding, of course."

"That's not the end I'm worried about. Daisy! Come!"

Instead of obeying, his dog moved a couple of steps closer to the blonde, who regarded him with a slight tilt of her head. "Does she always listen so well?"

"She usually listens." Whenever it worked to her advantage. "Then again, she's got a mind of her own. Typical woman."

"And what exactly is that supposed to mean?"

"That my dog is an independent thinker. More independent than I realized."

The woman's features softened as she looked at his dog. "Well, I can certainly respect that in any female. Even if she's invading my personal space."

He'd like to invade—

Dean cut off that thought before it could go any further. "I spotted your sweet ride from the road and stopped to see if you were in trouble." He jerked a thumb at the convertible behind him. "You're obviously not from around here. Are you having any problems?"

"Other than being accosted by a strange man and his dog? No."

"I was just trying to be nice."

"Thank you, but we're fine. I'd appreciate it if you'd go now."

We? He did a quick survey of the area and saw there was no one else around. Still, she'd made her feelings clear enough, so he should probably head out. Then again, there was something about her. Why did he get the feeling he might know—

"Hey! Cut it out!" The cultured air surrounding the lady disappeared the moment Daisy licked her bare leg, causing her to laugh. "That tickles!"

The husky sound and the smile on her lips sent a wave of pure desire straight through Dean; suddenly, getting his dog to listen was the last thing he cared about. For starters, he'd be happy if the woman would remove her sunglasses so he could see what color her eyes were.

"Stop that now." She scooted to one side, almost losing her footing in the sandy bottom of the river, but Daisy stayed right with her, a little pink tongue darting out again and again to lick at the water clinging to those gorgeous legs. "No more kisses, Miss Daisy. You need to behave."

Dumbfounded, Dean braced his hands on his hips and stared at his dog. What in the hell was going on?

Daisy was acting like a besotted fool. "Boy, I can honestly say I've never seen her act this way before."

The woman moved again, but the dog shadowed her every step. "Is that so?"

He crossed his arms over his chest, not sure if he liked this new side to his best friend. "Yeah, that's so."

"Well, if you don't mind, could you try calling her again?"

"I'll give it a shot." Dean dropped his arms and crouched to the ground, balancing on the balls of his feet. "Come on, Daisy, come here."

She didn't even spare him a glance. Nope, his dog wasn't the least bit interested in listening to him.

"Oh, for goodness' sake!" The woman headed his way

and his breath caught in his throat as he watched her walk, Daisy by her side. "As entertaining as this has been, it's time for you, Miss Daisy, to go back to your owner."

Daisy did start toward him, but then she turned back and let out a little yip as if she was disagreeing with her new friend, who laughed again. And this time, before Dean could get out another warning, she bent over and gently scratched behind the dog's ears.

Dean didn't know where to look first.

The enticing view of lace-covered curves thanks to the woman's gapping neckline or Daisy, who immediately plopped her butt in the shallow water and raised her snout, the picture of pure contentment.

He was unable to resist sneaking a second glance at the woman's sweet curves, before deciding to make a grab for his dog while she was distracted. Seconds later, he had Daisy in his arms, but when he straightened, the stranger did, too, and all it took was a bump of his shoulder against hers and down she went with a splash.

Ah, damn.

Trying to catch herself with her arms, she failed and fell backward, a soft cry falling from her lips. The water wasn't very deep, but she landed firmly on her backside, ending up waist-deep in the swift current. The sunglasses stayed in place and she managed to keep her face out of the water, but the rest of her—including most of her silky blond hair—was all wet.

"Whoa, sorry about that." Dean transferred Daisy into one hand and held her close to his chest, her wet fur drenching his shirt. With his other hand, he immediately reached for the woman. "Here, let me help."

"No!" Sputtering, she waved him away while trying to sit up. "No, thank you, I'm fine."

"Actually, what you are is soaking wet. Please, let me help you stand up."

She refused his hand again and somehow got to her feet. Her clothes now clung to her body, and thanks to the transparency of the wet material, every perfect inch of her, including her lacy bra and panties, were visible.

"Oh, I'm a mess!"

Dean wanted to argue that fact, but he doubted she'd be happy with him.

"I can't believe this!" she continued. "Look at me!"

He did his best to do just the opposite, but if something so beautiful was right in front of a man—

A low growl filled the air. Surprised, he looked down and found Daisy staring…at *him*. "Did you just growl at me, young lady?"

Clearly unhappy that he'd interrupted her fun, Daisy answered with another rumble that caused her entire body to vibrate.

"Is she okay?"

"Yeah, but I think she's a bit upset I came between the two of you," Dean said and then offered another smile. "And that I caused your tumble into the water. I really am sorry."

"Apology accepted, but if you don't mind…"

She left her sentence unfinished as she brushed past him. He turned to watch her retrieve a pair of high-heeled shoes and then head for her car.

Yep, the view was just as nice from this angle.

Dean followed, reaching her just as she leaned into the backseat of her convertible, grabbed a jacket and wiped at her face and arms. A quick glance into her side-view mirror had her clutching the jacket to her chest as she spun around.

"My clothes— The water—" she sputtered. "I look— You can see every—" She stomped her foot. "You just stood there!"

Daisy growled again as if confirming the lady's accusations. Not that Dean needed reminding. He was sure he would be dreaming about his run-in with this modern Aphrodite later tonight in the lonely confines of his bed. "Ah, look, is there anything I can do—"

"You can leave." Her upper-crust nature returned and her voice cooled as she shivered. "Now."

"I don't think I should leave you here alone—"

"I'm not alone. Snake!"

Snake? He glanced around, startled, but saw nothing on the ground nearby. When she called out again, he realized she wasn't talking about an actual reptile, but summoning someone.

What the hell? A bodyguard?

She certainly looked like the type who could afford paid protection, but where had the guy been for the past twenty minutes or so? Before Dean could ask, a tiny ball of fur raced out from the bushes, its yappy bark filling the air. The dog—if one could call it that—went straight to the lady and got between her and Dean, the annoying barking growing louder.

Daisy tensed, and Dean tightened his grip on her, but other than gazing intently at the little creature, his dog remained surprisingly silent.

"What is that?" he finally asked. "And does it have an off switch?"

"Hush, Snake. It's okay."

But still the little thing yipped away. Where had this pint-size terror been the whole time he'd been talking to her?

"What's he doing?" Dean asked. "Trying to act as tough as his name?"

"Actually, those are his initials. *S. N. A. K. E.* His full name is Sebastian Niles— Oh, Snake, hush!"

Dean couldn't stop himself from grinning at this sorry excuse for man's—or woman's—best friend. "Well, I see you have as much control of your pet as I do over mine— Hey!"

The dog had finally shut up, but only so it could focus on lifting one of its miniature back legs and peeing right on Dean's cowboy boot!

"Oh, my!" The feminine laughter started again before she suppressed it by pressing her fingertips to her lips. "Oh, I am sorry. Snake, come here."

The little rat trotted over and plopped down at its owner's feet.

"I do apologize," she repeated, the corners of those full lips turned upward. "Snake has never done anything like that before."

"Yeah, I'll bet." Dean gave his foot a quick shake. The bottom edge of his pant leg was now as damp as his shirt.

"Well, as you can see, I am very well guarded, so..."

"Okay, you win. We'll leave." He turned and headed for his truck. Tucking a finger beneath Daisy's chin, he made her look at him. "You know, if you just would've stayed in the truck..."

Opening the passenger door, he started to place Daisy inside, but held on to her instead and raised the window. Then he closed the door, walked around to the driver's side and climbed in. He made sure to hit the window lock before he released his dog into the passenger seat.

Sure enough, Daisy put her paw on the button.

"Oh, no, you've caused enough trouble for today." Dean scolded as he put the vehicle into gear and drove away, pausing to take a quick glance at the lady in his rearview mirror. "And thanks to you, I never even got her name."

Chapter Two

The Painted Lady Inn, a beautifully restored Victorian complete with turrets, gingerbread trim and a large wrap-around porch, was located on the east side of Destiny, which turned out to be a much smaller town than Priscilla anticipated. Intent on following the GPS directions and still a bit flustered from her encounter with the handsome stranger, she hadn't taken much time to look around as she made her way to her destination.

She'd seen brick-front businesses, many with colorful awnings and blooming flowers out front, surrounding a gazebo in the town's center green. It all looked a bit dated, but charming. There seemed to be more people on the side-walks than cars in the streets, and most turned to look as she drove past.

Pulling into the gravel lot next to the inn, Priscilla parked and locked her car, having raised the roof before leaving the river. She then walked inside with as much dignity as her appearance would allow, a small suitcase in one hand and Snake, this time with his leash attached, in the other.

She'd done her best to dry off before she got behind the wheel, tugging her jacket back on over her see-through dress and twisting her hair up again and clipping it in place, but she'd been unwilling to risk changing her clothes.

Who was to say another Good Samaritan wouldn't come along? One who'd also be well over six feet tall with powerfully built arms and a crazy dog?

She had to admit the stranger's size had been intimidating at first. She'd been wary of both him and his dog when he'd called out, but then the dog's exuberant greeting and wagging tail had won her over.

At least until she'd spotted the gleam of interest in the man's eyes.

That was the last thing she needed or wanted right now.

He'd done his best to be charming and she had to admit the dog was awfully cute, but then to find out just how sheer her pink silk tank top and skirt had become when wet—

"Hello, you must be Miss Lennox." A petite older woman with snow-white hair that brushed her shoulders and stylish gray glasses perched on her nose spoke from behind the counter on the other side of the front hall. "And I'm guessing this is your pet?"

"Yes, that's me." Suddenly exhausted, Priscilla was thankful the woman pointedly ignored her damp hair and clothes. She set her bag at her feet and shook the woman's hand. "And this is...well, he goes by his nickname, Snake."

Up went the lady's brows. "What an interesting moniker. I'm Minnie Gates, one of the owners of the Painted Lady. Welcome to our inn. We're glad to have both of you with us."

"Thank you." Having grown up in the hotel business, Priscilla could spot a person putting on airs a mile away, but this woman's charm and grace equaled that of her inn, making Priscilla feel instantly at home. "You have a beautiful place here."

"Thank you, we're quite proud of it." Minnie smiled and took Priscilla's credit card. Moments later she returned it along with an ornately fashioned key. "I've put you on the fourth floor. There are only two rooms up there and you're in our largest suite. If you'd like to head straight up, I can arrange to have the rest of your luggage brought to you."

Priscilla guessed she'd been watched as she parked, so the innkeeper would know she'd left her remaining cases in the backseat of her car. "That would be wonderful." She handed over her car keys, then spotted the small sign on the counter that listed spa services available at the inn. Just what she needed. A glance at her watch told her it was almost six o'clock. "Oh, a massage would be terrific after—well, after being behind the wheel all day. Is it too late to set one up?"

"If you can wait about thirty minutes, I should be able to arrange something for you."

"You're an angel, Ms. Gates."

"Please call me Minnie. All our spa services are done here on the main floor. Come down whenever you're ready."

Priscilla smiled her thanks, grabbed her bag and headed for the elevator. Once inside, she pulled Snake to her chest and graced him with a gentle kiss on his head. "Thank you for being a perfect gentleman with Minnie. I know the last couple of days have been rough and that scene down at the river didn't help."

Snake snuggled close and sighed. Priscilla remembered the first time the dog had done that. Her sister had brought the tiny creature home, presenting him with great fanfare, but then soon had gone off on another adventure, leaving Snake behind. A few days later the pup had followed Priscilla into her home office late one night. He'd weighed less than her briefcase when she picked him up and seconds later he'd made himself at home in her lap with the same contented sigh.

The elevator doors opened and Priscilla found her room at the end of the long hall. Stepping inside, she smiled as she took in the large space decorated in French country style. The bed linens, pillows and walls were done in soothing pastel colors such as aged ivory, lavender, pale yellow and green. The suite had a sitting area, complete with a fireplace on one side and a four-poster bed on the far wall. Her trained eye picked out the handmade, ornate Aubusson rug beneath her feet and the antique desk that sat directly in front of a set of windows that looked out over a beautiful garden and patio.

It didn't take long to get Snake settled before her luggage arrived. Then she pulled out her cell phone to charge it, noting she had two more messages from her father. That made six since she'd left Beverly Hills.

Forcing herself to enter her passcode, she listened to the last one he'd left for her around lunchtime today.

"Priscilla, where are you? It's been two days since the gala. An event you walked out on halfway through, I might add. I can't reach your sister, either, but that's no surprise. Call me. This situation needs to be handled. Now. This isn't like you. You know how much I count on you being the responsible one—"

Cutting off the message before he could finish his lecture, Priscilla noted her father sounded more angry than worried by the fact he couldn't seem to reach her.

She itched to return his call, to tell him someone else needed to handle things this time, but she'd already tried twice today and ended up leaving a message with his efficient secretary. She'd asked that he be told she was fine, still planned to be out of town for the foreseeable future and would call when she was settled.

Deciding that would do for now, she peeled off her damp clothes and slipped into a pair of dry panties, comfortable yoga sweats and a simple top. She hesitated for a moment, but then left her hair in the messy knot on her head and gave the large claw-foot bathtub in the adjoining bath a longing glance before realizing more than a half hour had passed and she was supposed to be downstairs.

First a massage, then she'd order some dinner from a local restaurant chosen from the list she'd found on the desk and crack open a gourmet doggy-food packet for Snake.

After all that, she should probably call Bobby and let him know—surprise!—she was in town.

She went downstairs and wandered around the first floor, walking through two beautiful parlors filled with comfortable antique furniture, fresh flowers and lots of books. But she didn't see her host anywhere.

"Can I help you?"

Priscilla turned and found the nice young girl who had brought her suitcases to her room earlier. "I'm looking for Minnie. She's arranged for me to have a massage and I fear I'm running late."

"Minnie has gone to the carriage house out back—that's where she and the Major live—but I can show you where to go if you like."

"Yes, please."

Priscilla followed the girl, who looked to still be in high school, back into the first parlor, when the old-fashioned ringing of a telephone filled the air. "Oh, I need to get that," she said. "If you just go to the room on the other side of the foyer with the double glass doors, you'll see everything is ready for you."

Heading in the direction the girl pointed, Priscilla found

a large ballroom on the other side of the foyer. It was empty, but she could easily picture it being used for parties and receptions. She walked deeper into the room, spotting the glass doors at the far end.

She stepped through them and found a converted porch with beautifully arched floor-to-ceiling windows that allowed light to pour in while honeycomb-shaped blinds assured privacy. A massage table draped in white linens had been set up in the center of the room with a nearby table holding scented candles, assorted lotions, a glass pitcher of ice water with sliced lemons and a stack of oversize towels.

Perfection.

No sign of the masseur or masseuse yet, but knowing she was already running late, Priscilla grabbed one of the towels and headed for the restroom in the far corner.

She quickly undressed and wrapped the towel around her. Leaving her clothes on a nearby chair, she headed for the table and perched herself on the edge, figuring she'd stretch out and wait. Before she could twist around to lie on her stomach, the glass doors opened.

"Sorry to keep you waiting." A deep male voice filled the air. "Boy, I've had the craziest afternoon—"

Priscilla froze when the sexy Good Samaritan from earlier today entered the room. "You!"

Confusion crossed his face for a moment as he studied her. Then he flashed her that same confident grin he'd sent her way earlier today. "Well, this is a nice surprise."

She couldn't believe it! Of all people, why would he be— "What are you doing here?"

"Ah, you'll have to forgive me for not recognizing you right away…." His voice trailed off as he took a step into the room, his gaze darting around the floor. "You look a little different without your sunglasses."

His perusal stopped the moment it landed on her bare toes and his smile deepened as he slowly let his gaze travel up her legs. By the time he reached the edge of the towel that rode high on her thighs, a warm flush had enveloped Priscilla.

She should be annoyed at his deliberate scrutiny, but for some reason she was—pleased? No, that couldn't be right. Just because her ex had rarely taken his nose out of his financial journals, even during a dinner conversation, didn't mean she thought that she felt—

"Or without your clothes," he added.

Okay, pleased or not, he shouldn't be in here. "Look, I don't know who you are—"

"Dean Zippenella." He moved to stand right in front of her and held out his hand. "We never got around to introductions down by the creek. At least, not the human kind."

Placing her hand in his was an automatic gesture, thanks to her years of philanthropic work, but the zing of sensation dancing across her palm the moment they touched was new and totally unexpected.

She tried to draw her hand back. Too late.

His fingers closed around hers and held tight as he took another step toward her. This close, she could see the touch of gray in his closely cropped dark hair; the stubble on his jaw was the same dark color. A mix of sage, suede and musk invaded her nose, a spicy scent that must be his cologne. Despite sitting on the table, she had to tilt her head back to look at him, something that didn't happen often, seeing as how she was just a few inches shy of six feet tall.

Without her heels.

Priscilla gave a gentle tug, a universal signal it was past time for him to release her, but his gaze flicked down over her shoulders and the exposed upper curves of her breasts, pausing for a heartbeat there before returning to her face.

"And you are?" he asked.

Her other hand involuntarily tightened where it kept hold of the towel's overlapping edges. He didn't look like the sort who would attack a woman, much less someone who read gossip magazines, but would he recognize her name? Would that make any difference?

"Priscilla Lennox," she answered after a pause.

"It's nice to meet you, Priscilla." No flicker of recognition crossed his face at the sound of her name as he finally released her. "And please, let me apologize again for earlier today."

He sounded sincere, but that still didn't explain why he was here. "Apology already accepted. You didn't have to chase me down—"

"I didn't, even though I was glad to see your car in the inn's parking lot. I'm here for an appointment."

She noticed he'd changed his clothes. Gone were the khaki trousers and collared shirt he'd had on earlier. He now wore a simple black T-shirt that hugged his chest and shoulders, the word *ARMY* spelled out in big block letters across the front. Well-worn jeans, faded in some interesting places, and black boots— Wait, did he just say appointment? He looked more like a member of a motorcycle club than a masseur, but in a town this size…

She sighed, accepting that fate wasn't quite done messing with her yet. "Well, I guess I'm that appointment."

His left eyebrow shot up. "Excuse me?"

She had no idea why he looked so surprised. But they might as well just make the best of it. In a much-practiced move, Priscilla stretched out on the table and turned over on her stomach, all the while keeping the towel securely in place.

Resting her suddenly pounding forehead on her folded hands, she closed her eyes and said, "Just get started, please."

Dean had to admit he wanted nothing more than to get his hands on this beautiful creature, but not like this. Obviously, Priscilla Lennox thought he was here to provide a massage, a service contracted by the inn, but she must've gotten her rooms mixed up.

This area was reserved for his weekly appointments with the retired marine who owned the inn. The old man hated hospitals so much he refused to come to the veterans' clinic where Dean worked for his physical-therapy sessions. Considering the hell the still-spry veteran had gone through as a prisoner of war in Vietnam, Dean believed he'd more than earned the right to feel any damn way he pleased.

So every Friday afternoon Dean—being former military himself—ended his work week here at the inn, in a less clinical setup.

He'd noticed the familiar red convertible when he'd arrived at the inn and hoped for the chance to run into the pretty blonde again and make a second and better impression this time. But not this way. "Ah, look, I think I should explain about the massage—"

"No, you look. No more explanations. No more apologies." She propped herself on her elbows, glaring at him over one shoulder, the move causing a single blond curl to fall across her blue eyes. Very beautiful blue eyes. "I've had a really long day, after what has been a terrible—a terribly exhausting week. Getting knocked on my butt into a riverbed earlier didn't help."

Dean kept his boots planted firmly tableside, forcing his gaze to remain on her face when he caught sight of the edges of her towel slowly giving way. He'd noticed the yellow rosebud tattoo just above the towel's edge a moment ago, but now her jerky movements were leaving even more of her curves on display.

"All I want is for you to work out the kinks," she continued, her tone clipped, "and if you could manage to do that in silence, that would be preferable."

Well, if Miss High Society got that pretty little nose any higher in the air, she might just topple backward off the table.

Dean glanced at his watch. It wasn't like the Major to be running late. He was sure the old man was going to show up before he even got his hands on her.

He bowed slightly. "Your wish is my command, Miss Lennox."

Pursing her lips together, she eyed him in silence. He was sure she was going to say something else, but instead she went back to her prone position.

Dean rubbed his hands together, eyeing the perfection of her porcelain skin. His trained gaze picked up on the tension in her neck and her shoulders. The woman did look as if she could use a good rubdown. It would serve her right if he peeled that towel right to the edge of the swell of her nicely shaped backside so he'd have plenty of room to touch all her interesting spots.

Flexing his fingers, he reached out—

The clicking of the Major's cane against the glass door announced his arrival only seconds before his booming voice filled the air. "Sorry to be late to the ball game, son. The kitchen sink went FUBAR on me and the damn wrench broke— Oh, excuse me, ma'am."

This time Priscilla jumped, lifting herself up on her elbows as she snapped them to her sides.

Dean laid a hand against the plush terry material in the

center of her back, holding her in place. "I wouldn't do that if I were you," he said, keeping his voice low.

Her head whipped around. She glared at him. "What—what is going on?"

"Have I interrupted something?" Elwin Gates asked. "I didn't mean to walk in unannounced."

"No worries, sir," Dean answered. "Just a slight mix-up."

Keeping his back to the old man, Dean reached for the terry robe draped over a nearby chair. The Major usually donned it after their session, but Dean had a feeling Miss Lennox needed it more at this very minute.

"Why don't you rise slowly, facing the other way, and slip into this?" Dean continued to speak in quiet tones, holding up the robe for her. "And *then* maybe you'll let me explain?"

Her eyes narrowed, but she rotated away from him, grabbing at the towel and tucking the ends in place again as she rose up on one hip. He laid the robe across her shoulders and waited as she slipped her arms inside. The terry material pooled as she sat upright, then flowed around her thighs when she slipped off the far side of the table.

Dean turned around and found the Major standing in the doorway, a grin on his wrinkled face. He offered the old man a quick wink. "Are you all set, Miss Lennox?"

"Y-yes, thank you."

He looked back over one shoulder, watching as she stepped around the table, head held high as if she were wearing a ball gown instead of an oversize robe.

Dean made the introductions. "This is one of your guests, Priscilla Lennox. I'm afraid she mistook this room for the one used for spa services provided here at the inn. Miss Lennox, this is Major General Elwin Gates, United States Marine Corps, Retired, and proprietor of the Painted Lady. He's here for his physical-therapy session."

"It's very nice to meet you, sir." She stepped forward, offered a bright smile and held out her hand. "I do apologize for my error and for taking over your private session."

"Apologies aren't necessary, miss." Elwin returned her handshake. "And you can call me Major. Everyone does. Now, I'm going to see where my wife disappeared to so we can get you to the right place."

"Oh, you don't have to leave on my account. I'll just gather my clothes and let you two gentlemen get to your session."

She backed up a few steps and walked right into Dean. He grabbed her waist to steady her, but she whirled around, the sweet politeness replaced with a contemptuous look that had him holding up both hands in mock surrender.

"Hey, I tried to tell you."

"You didn't try very hard," she retorted, her voice low.

"You don't have to whisper. Major's gone to find out where your massage is *supposed* to be taking place."

"That's fine, but I'm leaving, as well."

She tried to sidestep around him, but Dean latched on to her arm. "Hold on. You're not going anywhere yet."

"Oh, I'm not?" Her eyes turned icy, but the toss of her head and the squaring of her shoulders told him a little spitfire lay inside this cool beauty. Dean liked that.

"Look, we've gotten off on the wrong foot. Twice." He eased his hold, his fingers gently massaging the inside of her elbow through the material. "Let me make it up to you. Have you eaten? We could grab something after our respective appointments."

"I'm not—"

A low rumbling interrupted her. She slapped her free hand over her stomach.

He grinned.

Women like Priscilla Lennox—classy, wealthy, high society—were way out of his league. A lesson he'd learned the hard way a few years back before he'd moved out west to Destiny from his home in Sea Point, New Jersey.

Heck, he'd bet her car cost more than what he'd spent on his couple of acres of land north of town and the log home he'd had built there last year. But he'd been spending too much time alone lately and it didn't hurt to hit one for the fences every now and then. And Daisy actually seemed to like her.

"You were saying?"

She lifted her chin. "I'm not hungry."

"You sure I can't tempt you with the best burgers this side of the Rockies? The Blue Creek Saloon has great food, cold beer, and on Friday nights there's usually a band playing kick-ass country music. It's not as fancy as what you're probably used to, but I think you'd enjoy it."

The icy veneer in her eyes spread to her entire body. She pulled free of his hold. "As interesting as that sounds, Mr. Zippenella, I plan to stay in tonight."

He liked the sound of his name on her lips, and she even pronounced it correctly. She was also turning him down.

He watched her walk toward the chair where her clothes lay neatly folded. "Another night, perhaps."

She took the pile in her arms and then headed for the door. "I'm aware Destiny is a small town, but I don't see any reason for us to run into each other again."

Hmm, what was that old proverb his *nonni* always used to say? *May you be wise enough to know when to give up the fight.* Of course, the words sounded prettier in her native Italian, and it'd been advice he and his brothers had rarely followed. "How long do you plan to be in town?"

"I don't really know." She paused in the doorway. "It really depends on the man I came here to see."

A man. And just like that his attempt at a home run fizzled as the third strike whizzed by him. She was in town because of a man.

Chapter Three

"Your place is truly spectacular, Bobby." Priscilla sat at one end of an outdoor sectional sofa, which, along with a pair of matching chairs, defined the entertainment area of an oversize back deck that ran the length of the massive log home. Set in a lush forest on the side of a mountain, the house had taken Priscilla's breath away when she'd first pulled into the circular drive. "Both inside and out. The pictures in the magazines don't do it justice."

"Thank you." The former race-car champion set about fixing drinks behind the bar while his wife, Leeann, set a tray of cheese, crackers and fruit on the glass coffee table. "I've dreamed of living in a log house since I was kid, so when I finally had the money to do it right—"

"He went a bit overboard." Leeann cut off her husband with a smile as she curled up in the opposite corner of the sofa. "As usual."

"Lee didn't like the place when she first saw it."

"Hey, I said it was impressive."

"Which was her polite way of saying lifeless." Bobby joined them, handing each woman a glass of iced tea. Then he motioned at Priscilla's purse. "You sure your friend doesn't need anything? Maybe some water?"

Priscilla took a quick peek inside the oversize tote tucked next to her, happy to see Snake curled up asleep. "No, I think the tour wore him out. Even with you carrying him from room to room most of the time."

Bobby grinned and reached back for an icy beer he'd left on the bar for himself and then sat next to his wife, wrapping his arm around her. "I felt bad for the guy, trying to keep up on those little legs. And Lee was right. The place was impressive, but sterile. After I won her heart—again—she added life, and love, and made it a home for us."

Priscilla smiled as the couple shared a quick kiss. It was easy to see Bobby was truly happy, which hadn't always been the case in the years before a spectacular crash had ended his successful racing career.

"Well, you've succeeded in creating a warm and inviting home. Leeann, I'm so glad we got the chance to meet and that I could see your place in person."

"We're happy to show it off, but now that the tour is over, you still haven't said how you ended up in our little corner of the world." Bobby took a quick swallow from his beer. "Did I tell you how surprised I was to get your call? Not to mention to hear that you were right here in Destiny. The last time we saw each other was just before my accident, when you and Jonathan hosted that charity-sailing gig down in San Diego."

Priscilla tried not to squirm on the sofa—Lennox women never squirmed, according to her father—at Bobby mentioning her ex. No, Bobby hadn't come right out and said he'd been surprised by the breakup, but the disbelief in his voice had been evident when they'd spoken last night.

After that embarrassing mix-up over who exactly was supposed to be giving her a massage, and where, Priscilla had gone through with the appointment, not wanting to waste the time of the woman who had indeed been waiting for her in another part of the inn. She then made her way back to her room, blaming the warmth flowing through her veins and the tingling sensation dancing over her skin on the well-executed bodywork. That had to be the reason. It couldn't possibly be because she'd actually wondered for a moment or two during the massage what it would've felt like to have that Good Samaritan/physical therapist/shameless flirt be the one to pull, tug and rub her sore muscles.

Or if she should have accepted his dinner invitation.

Her stomach had certainly liked the idea, but his crack about the local restaurants not being up to the level of what she might be used to set off warning bells. Had he figured out who she was? Of course, it would only take a quick Google search to find out what she'd been through the past week. "Priscilla?"

She blinked, realizing Bobby and Leeann were waiting for her to answer. What was the question again? Oh, yes. Why she was in town.

"Well, my vacation plans for the summer changed rather suddenly." Priscilla paused to wet her dry throat with a sip of tea. Priscilla had wondered if her family's latest escapade with the Hollywood gossip mill was something Bobby would mention when she arrived, but neither he nor Leeann had said anything as they welcomed her warmly into their home. "When I found myself taking a spontaneous road trip, I decided to head somewhere…unexpected."

"I guess Destiny could be considered that, considering your usual surroundings," Leeann said. "We're about as far away from the glitz and glamour of Beverly Hills as one can get."

Priscilla heard no malice in the woman's tone, but she was thankful for the years of experience that kept her smile relaxed. She did feel a bit lost and out of place in this small Western town, much like Alice when she'd dropped into Wonderland.

Not to mention the fact she was vastly overdressed.

Her deep purple silk sundress and favorite taupe-colored peep-toed heels were a bit much for a casual Saturday afternoon. Despite her friend Lisa's hairstyle suggestion, she'd gone with her familiar French twist and simple yet elegant gold jewelry. She carried a leather tote big enough for her portfolio, not to mention Snake and his favorite pillow.

After going through her suitcases this morning, she'd realized that while her wardrobe might be perfect for a European holiday, most of her outfits wouldn't fit into the much more casual style of a place like Destiny, Wyoming.

Bobby's wife, a stunning brunette who moved with an ease that spoke of her former career as a fashion model, wore a simple outfit of dark blue shorts that ended just above her knees, a white cotton shirt and canvas sneakers with no laces. Bobby, too, was dressed casually in jeans and a T-shirt embroidered with his former team's racing logo.

She couldn't remember one time during her three years with Jonathan when he'd ever worn a shirt without a collar. Not even last summer while cruising on his yacht.

"Yes, well, getting away—" Priscilla hesitated and then pushed any thoughts of her ex from her head "—is exactly what I…planned. Now, why don't you tell me more about this summer camp of yours? You mentioned it when you showed me the architectural drawings and photographs in your study, but I'd love to hear more."

"This is the first summer Camp Diamond has been open,

so we consider it a shakedown period," Bobby said. "The staff is pretty much in place and we've offered free stays for local kids from Destiny in return for acting as test subjects, for lack of a better word, for two-week sessions that will run through Labor Day. We'll take a week off in between each session to make any needed repairs, upgrades or rework any of the programs."

While Bobby spoke, Priscilla leaned over and placed her glass on the low square table in front of her and then reached for her portfolio. She itched to start making notes, but held off until she could gauge how he and Leeann were going to feel about her research. "How's that working?"

"Well, we're only finishing up the first week of our second session, but so far, so good." He glanced at his wife, who offered a nod in agreement. "A few hiccups along the way, but we expected that. The plan is to have our first full season next summer."

"We have a business plan, a board of directors and an advisory council for the camp in place, as well," Leeann added. "Thanks to my husband's generosity, Camp Diamond doesn't carry any debt on its land or the buildings, and it's fully funded for the next few years."

Hmm, she hadn't been aware of that fact. "It must take quite a bit of financial support to run this type of operation year after year, covering everything from salaries to insurance to marketing. Is raising funds an important part of your business plan?"

"Ah, yes, it is, but like Lee said, we're in a good place money-wise at the moment." Bobby paused. "Wait a minute. Have you been looking into this?"

Priscilla smiled, glad that he seemed more surprised than insulted at her initiative. "It's what I do, remember?"

"Yeah, I know, but I never expected… Wow. I only mentioned the camp a couple of times when you called to thank me for our donation to your gala event this past week."

It took a bit of effort, but she managed to keep the tainted images from that night from coming back to life and focused instead on the here and now. "I was intrigued by what you're trying to do."

"Talk about great timing," Leeann said, enthusiasm shining in her eyes. "We were just trying to come up with ideas for a fund-raising event and here we have an expert right in front of us."

Taking that as permission to proceed, Priscilla flipped open her portfolio and glanced at her notes. "So, have you thought about corporate sponsorship?"

"We do have one—my former racing team that I'm still a part owner of—but I'm a bit hesitant about having outsiders giving funds and then wanting a voice in how the camp is run."

Priscilla added the information about Bobby's team to the list she'd created this morning. "What about sponsors a bit closer to home?"

"Well, there aren't exactly a lot of big corporations in Destiny."

A fact she knew thanks to her research, but Priscilla had something different in mind. "What I meant was maybe you should be looking at people who have a connection to this area instead of looking for business sponsors."

Bobby glanced at his wife for a moment, then looked back at Priscilla. "That's sort of what we have in mind when it comes to an event, but I'm guessing you're talking about people with deep pockets?"

"Exactly." Priscilla pulled out her list. "Have either of you ever heard of the high-tech mogul Drake Hamill?"

"Sure. Bill Gates, Steve Jobs, Drake Hamill. They're all members of the same club."

"Drake and his company are based in Silicon Valley, but he's originally from Laramie. He attended the University of Wyoming and has a vacation home in Jackson Hole, so he comes back to the state often."

"I've met him a few times at your foundation events in L.A.," Bobby said. "We did talk about being from Wyoming. Interesting idea."

"I found that long-established camps often rely on alumni, not only to send their children to the same camp they once attended, but to assist in fund-raising efforts, as well. You don't have that yet, but there used to be a summer camp in town that ran for over twenty-five years. Their former campers might be interested in learning there's a new camp here in Destiny."

Bobby nodded. "I guess that's something we could look into. If we can get any information from the Shipmans, the family that used to own the old camp."

"It would take a bit of doing," Leeann added. "There aren't any Shipmans still living in Destiny that I know of."

"Well, I've found at least one former camper who's a big name. Did you know that the San Antonio Alamos' second baseman, Jax Summers, was born and raised in Chapman Falls, which is only two hours from here? According to his website, he first learned to hit a baseball while attending the Shipmans' camp. His parents still live up there and he's often home during the off season."

Bobby looked impressed. "I don't think I ever knew that."

"I've come up with a half-dozen people who have a history of generous charitable giving and, most importantly, a connection to this area."

"Can we see that list?" Bobby asked.

Priscilla handed them her findings, watching as Bobby and Leeann, heads close together, read it.

She was pleased that her ideas were going over so well. As someone whose closest experience to kids' summer camp was English riding lessons at the Beverly Hills Riding Club, Priscilla had spent a lot of time over the past few days learning everything she could about summer camps.

She'd been surprised to find ones that specialized in everything from sports to technology to the arts, but she'd concentrated on private, traditional sleepaway camps that offered a variety of activities like Camp Diamond.

"I think you're onto something here." Bobby tapped a finger against the piece of paper. "This is an idea the board of directors should explore further, but when Leeann said we were looking at fund-raising, we were actually thinking of something simpler."

"Simpler?"

"And even more local." Leeann rested a hand on Bobby's jean-clad thigh. "From the very beginning, we wanted the people of Destiny, our families and friends, to be a part of the camp. We used a local company, Murphy Mountain Log Homes, to design and build all the buildings, and while we had to go outside the area to fill some of the senior staff positions, a lot of the staff, including most of the counselors, are local high-school and college kids."

"Yes, well, I'm sure summer jobs are scarce in a town this small, so that's a good thing, but I'm not sure what you're looking for as far as—"

"Hey! Anyone home?"

A deep, booming voice filled the air, cutting her off. It seemed to come through the trees, but Priscilla guessed whoever bellowed was down below the wraparound deck.

"Yeah, we're here. Come on up," Bobby called out and then offered a sheepish grin when his wife swatted at him. "Sorry about that, Priscilla. A buddy of mine is here for an early dinner. Why don't you stay and join us?"

"Oh, I don't want to intrude."

"You won't. Please stay," Leeann said. "We have plenty of food and this way I won't be outnumbered. As usual."

"Hey, you're never outnumbered."

"A female dog doesn't count— Oh, no! Bobby, he's got Dais—"

A blur of wiry golden-and-brown hair on four legs raced around the corner of the deck. Before Priscilla could brace herself, she had a familiar furry snout pressed into her hand as the same dog that greeted her yesterday in the river jumped up on the sectional right next to her.

Which meant her owner wasn't too far behind.

"Oh, my, would you look at that." Leeann's voice was low. "I never thought I'd see this day."

Priscilla's hand stilled where she spontaneously started to scratch at the dog's ears. She looked up and found Leeann and Bobby staring, mouths agape. "I'm sorry?"

"That dog hates women," Leeann said, "but look at her cuddling up to you."

"I don't think I've ever seen Daisy behave this way before," Bobby added.

"Tell me about it."

Priscilla turned sharply at the familiar voice, instantly recognizing her Good Samaritan and Daisy's owner.

The first thing she saw was a pair of battered deck shoes. Her gaze slowly rose over tanned muscular legs dusted with dark hairs to his baggy cargo shorts. His deep green Camp Diamond T-shirt was untucked and stretched taut across his broad, powerful chest.

When a knowing grin crossed his handsome face, Priscilla realized she'd just assessed him as closely as he'd done to her yesterday. At least he was wearing more than a towel.

Too bad.

Surprised at the thoughts racing through her mind and

the way her body responded to them, Priscilla forced her gaze to remain locked with the man she hadn't thought she'd see again. "Well, hello."

He bowed slightly and tipped his head, and she couldn't tell if he meant the gesture to be gallant or mocking. "Hello to you. Again."

"Wait, you two know each other?" Bobby asked.

Priscilla turned back, rushing to speak before Dean could. "We met yesterday afternoon when I first arrived in town."

"Down by the Blue Creek. She was pulled over and I stopped to see if she needed any help."

"Yes, Mr. Zippenella and his dog were quite the welcoming committee," she hastily added, hoping Dean wouldn't mention the details of their run-in, both in the water and later at the inn.

"To say Daisy is smitten is a bit of an understatement," the man added, walking toward the bar.

"Boy, I'd say. Look at her. She's never been that friendly with me or any woman in town." Leeann's voice was still filled with awe. "What's your secret?"

"I don't quite understand it, either." Priscilla found herself once again moving her fingertips along the dog's neck. "I mean, I'm a fan of animals, of course, but even I was a bit surprised at how outgoing—"

"Yeah, speaking of animals, where's that pint-size yip factory of yours?" Dean asked. "What did you call it? Snack?"

Priscilla glanced at her bag, surprised the pup hadn't made an appearance yet. "*Snake* is taking a nap at the moment— Oh!"

His tiny pointed ears popped up first, and then seconds later, Snake hopped from his hiding spot and landed on the deck at Priscilla's feet. The dog growled deep in his throat, causing Daisy's owner to slide onto one of the tall stools situated in front of the bar.

And lift his feet well out of reach.

Dean's favorite deck shoes had been through hell over the years, and they looked it, but they'd never been peed on. The last thing he wanted was for that rat to get a second shot at him.

"Snake. Hush!"

This time the pup listened to his owner.

Dean took a moment to pull in a deep breath, watching Priscilla lean over and easily lift her pet to her side.

The last person he'd expected to run into here was Miss Lennox.

When she'd told him yesterday she was in town to meet up with a man, he'd never thought in a million years it'd be Bobby. Of course, she did look like the type of woman his buddy had dated over the years once his racing career had taken off. Blonde. Beautiful. Bankrolled. That was before Bobby had returned to Destiny and rekindled his high-school love affair with Leann a couple of years ago.

You're about eighteen months too late, honey.

Dean thought back to Bobby and Leann's wedding, held right here in their home on New Year's Eve. He'd stood up as best man for them, having gotten Bobby back on his feet with an innovative physical-therapy program that had led to Dean's employment with the local veterans' center.

Sticking around and becoming a permanent resident of Destiny hadn't been in his plans. He'd always figured he'd head back to his native New Jersey, but he'd found something here in this quiet rural community that had been missing in his life.

"Well, I guess Priscilla's dog doesn't feel the same way about you, huh, buddy?" Bobby asked, then grinned.

"Tell me about it." Dean looked back at Priscilla, who'd managed to quiet her pet. "You think I can get myself a beer without being attacked?"

"Oh, you'll be safe," she answered, her smile confident. She continued to pet both dogs as they played at rubbing noses before settling into curled balls of fur on either side of her. "As long as you stay over there."

"Yeah, I bet." Deciding it was best to move slowly, Dean eased off the stool and walked behind the bar. He pulled a cold beer from the refrigerator and popped the top as curiosity got the best of him. Would Bobby really invite an ex-girlfriend to town? "So, how do you all know each other?"

"Priscilla is visiting from Los Angeles. She's got some great ideas for fund-raising for the camp."

"I didn't know you were looking into that." Dean figured the princess could easily write a check to pay the camp's bills for the next year without breaking a nail. "So, you're a moneymaker?"

She lifted her chin and her blue eyes regarded him snootily. "I generate philanthropic support for a wide variety of nonprofit organizations, so yes, I guess 'moneymaker' is an apt title."

There was that spitfire he'd caught a glimpse of yesterday. "So, what kind of support are you dreaming up for the camp?"

"Well, we just started talking about what Bobby and Leeann have in mind for an event." She looked back at them. "Based on my experience, I could offer any number of ideas for an intimate gathering, from a plated dinner to an art auction, perhaps?"

"Plated dinners around here are potlucks, and the closest thing we have to art is the craft fair at the local high school." Dean took a long swallow from his beer, wondering why he was goading her.

Maybe because she was one of Bobby's former flames?

If so, thanks to the unwritten male code, she would be off-limits to any of the let's-get-to-know-each-other-better ideas that had swirled around inside his head from the moment he'd met her. "You're going to have to get more creative than that."

Both Bobby and Leeann shot him dark looks, his friend's laced with confusion, while Leann's was downright pissed.

"Those are both great ideas, but like I started to say before we were interrupted—" Leeann's tone softened as she turned to her guest "—we're looking for more than just a standard fund-raiser. Everyone in Destiny has embraced the idea of the camp. Many are asking how they can help, but we don't want to just take their money."

"You want to accept their contributions during a specific event for the community that will earmark any funds as going directly to the camp. I totally understand that." Priscilla finished Leann's sentence, taking her attention off the dogs and scribbling on the notepad on her lap. "Give me a moment, won't you?"

Silence filled the air and Dean could almost see the wheels turning inside Priscilla's head. He caught his friends looking his way again, but he kept his gaze on Priscilla's perfectly coiffed hair, deciding he preferred it long and loose around her shoulders like when he first saw her down at the river. Or wet and streaming down her back as it had been when she'd risen from the water.

He wondered what this society princess was going to come up with that would appeal to the folks of Destiny. Then she scratched over whatever she'd just written with firm strokes, repeating that three times and then circling the last item on her list.

"Now, I'm not sure how well this idea would work. It really depends on a variety of factors related to the town, starting of course with a willingness to go for something a bit unconventional…." Her words were soft, almost as if she were talking aloud to herself. She then looked up at Dean. "Are you a bachelor, Mr. Zippenella?"

Surprised by her question, the beer bottle almost slipped from his fingers. Did she really think he'd hit on her if he was married? He tightened his grip. "Didn't I make that fact clear yesterday?"

A light flush colored her cheeks. "Yes, you did. My apologies."

Bobby laughed. "Are you kidding? Zip will be one of Destiny's last bachelors."

One elegant eyebrow lifted. "Zip?"

For a reason he couldn't figure out at the moment, Dean didn't want her calling him that. "It's a nickname. But call me Dean."

She blinked once, the pink tinge on her face deepening as she focused her attention back on Bobby and Leeann. "Would you say that the single-to-married ratio is fairly balanced in Destiny?"

"I guess so," Leeann answered. "I never really thought about it much."

"What about male versus female? I'm hoping Mr. Zipp—Dean—isn't truly the town's last bachelor?"

"Oh, yeah?" Dean asked. "Why is that?"

"Well, you would need at least a dozen to make this worthwhile."

"I'm confused," Bobby said. "A dozen what?"

"Bachelors," Priscilla announced with a bright smile. "A bachelor auction, with the ladies bidding for a night on the town with the men of their choice, could be just the event you're looking for."

Chapter Four

The surprise in Priscilla's blue eyes told him laughter was the last thing she expected in response to her idea, but Dean—and thankfully, Bobby was chuckling right there with him—couldn't help himself. "Are you serious?" he choked out after pausing to catch his breath. "Okay, I'm sorry. I can see you are, but a bachelor auction? That's—"

"Wonderful!" Leeann scooched to the edge of the sofa and leaned toward Priscilla. "I think it's a perfectly wonderful idea."

"You do?" Dean and Bobby spoke in unison.

Bobby's amusement instantly faded to disbelief. "Really?"

"Of course!" She turned to her husband, staring at him as if she didn't understand how he didn't see the big picture. "There are plenty of unmarried men in Destiny who can participate. Many of the ranches must have single cowboys. Heck, Maggie and Landon have expanded their place so much over the last year they've got at least three or four men who are unattached."

"Does that include Willie? He's got to be pushing eighty," Bobby said. "Hey, wait a minute, you said you've never thought about the unmarried men in this town."

"I haven't. Until now. And yes, Willie could be included. There shouldn't be an age limit. What about the sheriff's department? I've been away a few years now, but I know there's at least a couple of single—" Leeann broke off, turning back to Priscilla. "Divorced men count, too, right? Single dads are okay?"

"Uh, yeah, sure." Priscilla looked surprised by the question, but then she recovered. "I mean, of course, divorced men and single dads would be fine. Being currently unattached would be the only prerequisite, I'd imagine."

"Do you really think ladies are going to bid on a man?" Dean asked, the whole concept a bit mind-boggling for him. He was all for the female sex taking the initiative, but this? "For a date?"

"Are you kidding? They'll love it. It's like the old Sadie Hawkins dances back in high school! You remember? Where the girls get to invite the boys?" Leeann asked.

"How could I forget? It was one of our first dates," Bobby said. "Of course, that invite didn't cost you anything."

"Just a lot of sleepless nights and a healthy chunk of my teenage pride over the fear you'd say no. Now, where to hold such an event?" Leeann paused, biting down on her bottom lip for a moment. "We would need a place big enough— Oh, I know! The Blue Creek Saloon! It's a big place with a huge dance floor and a stage. Would that work?"

Priscilla glanced his way for a moment. Was she remembering his offer of the best burgers in town, maybe?

"I don't know what the facility looks like, but a stage

would work best for this sort of event," she said. "Perhaps a runway could be constructed? The ladies could sit on either side while the bachelors walk back and forth?"

"Oh, a runway would be perfect." Leeann said with a grin. "Let the buyers get a good look at what they're spending their money on."

"Hey, you sure about this?" Bobby reached for his wife's hand and held fast. "I wouldn't want the auction to bring back any memories…you know, a runway? Modeling?"

"Don't worry, honey. I'll be fine."

Dean was glad to hear Leeann say that, even if his buddy didn't look entirely convinced. In her former life, Leeann had been a famous fashion model, but a terrible experience at a photo shoot had made her give up her career. She'd eventually returned to Destiny and worked as a deputy for the sheriff's department, but had left the force just before Bobby and Dean came to town. Now she was committed full-time to the camp.

"I'm serious," Leeann continued, punctuating her words with a kiss for her husband. "That's behind me now. Let's concentrate on the fund-raiser, okay?"

"You know, you could also involve some of the other local restaurants." Priscilla scribbled in her notebook again. "Perhaps they could have a special menu in place for the week following the auction geared toward the winners and their dates. Or provide a coupon for a two-for-one dinner or a discount."

"That's a great idea. We'd have to get the okay from Racy—she's the owner of the Blue Creek— but if anyone will jump on board with this idea, it's Racy," Leeann added. "But when do we hold the event? I believe Racy books her bands a few weeks in advance, so we might be looking at August. That would give us plenty of time for planning and advertising. Can you stick around that long?"

"Stick around?" Priscilla asked.

"Sure. We'll need you here to coordinate the entire event, since it was your brainchild."

Dean had been listening to the back-and-forth about this crazy idea, waiting for the right moment to remind them that without the men agreeing to participate, this whole thing was going nowhere. He'd been about to say something when Leeann's question caused the conversation to fade into silence.

"I—ah—I hadn't thought that far," Priscilla finally said before she dropped her gaze to the notebook on her lap and flipped it closed. "I was just sharing a few thoughts off the top of my head."

"And the auction is the best one! We wanted something new and different, something that everyone in the town could be involved in. But we need a person with your experience to pull this together and to be the master of ceremonies."

"Oh, no, that's not my style." She looked up, her pen clenched tight in her fist. "I'm very much a behind-the-scenes kind of person."

Her words were softly spoken, but firm. Dean found her argument hard to believe. Someone as beautiful as her not wanting to be the center of attention?

"The host for the evening should be a person familiar with the locals, both the bachelors and the ladies doing the bidding," Priscilla continued. "Just in case either group is a bit shy about getting the ball rolling, which can happen at auctions. An added bonus would be someone who is also a big part of the camp. You would be perfect for the job, Leeann."

"Me?" Leeann flattened one hand against her chest. "Well, yeah, I guess I could...but only if you're here to help me. Please? You did say your plans for the summer changed. Do you have the free time? Can you stay?"

Dean found himself holding his breath, waiting for her to answer. Realizing how dumb that was, he purposely released it and took another long pull from his beer. Still, he couldn't look away, and when Priscilla released a soft sigh, he felt it all the way to his bones.

She was staying.

"Yes, of course I'll stay."

Leeann clapped her hands, joyous that she'd gotten her way. Not that Dean had had any doubt. When his buddy's wife wanted something, she usually got it. "I know you've taken a room at the inn, but you're welcome to move into one of our guest rooms if you and Snake would be more comfortable."

Dean's hand froze, the beer bottle halfway to his mouth. Priscilla stay here? Was Leeann nuts? Who invited their husband's ex-girlfriend to room down the hall?

Mind your own business. You aren't interested, remember?

Yeah, if he kept telling himself that, maybe he'd believe it. No, what Dean needed to keep telling himself was that the lady was off-limits thanks to his buddy having been there first. Even if the two of them hooking up had to have been at least three or four years ago. Right around the time he'd been getting shown the door by—

"Thank you for the invitation," Priscilla said, "but I think I'll—we'll—stay where we are."

"We all love the Painted Lady, and the house is a national landmark, but it must be vastly different from what you're used to."

Priscilla tucked her notebook away in her oversize bag and leaned forward to take her glass from the table. Straightening, she crossed one knee over the other, causing her skirt to ride up. Dean now had a perfect view of those magnificent legs that had haunted his dreams last night.

"Oh, the room is beautiful and quite large," she said. "I'm on the top floor and the staff has been very accommodating."

Dean snorted, then covered it up with a quick cough when she glanced his way. He bet they were accommodating. Major hadn't shut up about her the entire time Dean had put him through his paces during their physical-therapy session, grilling him about the beautiful blonde like the marine boot-camp drill sergeant he'd once been.

"Oh, you're in the best room at the inn. The bridal suite."

The smile remained, but she gripped her glass with both hands, her fingers pressed hard enough to turn her knuckles white. "Am I? I hadn't realized. Well, it's a comfortable room, large enough for me and Snake. Not to mention the claw-foot bathtub is a dream."

Okay, that was a visual he didn't need.

"I hate to throw a wrench into this whole auction idea—" Bobby nudged at his wife's shoulder "—but you still need to secure a group of men willing to be sold like cattle at a livestock auction. Thankfully, this side of beef is off the market."

"Yes, you are—" Leeann leaned in and gave him another quick kiss "—but you're right. Without the men, this isn't going to work. There are plenty to choose from, but getting them to agree might be another issue."

"Surely once you explain the reason behind the event they'd be willing to participate," Priscilla said. "At least for one date with the lady who wins him."

"Maybe, but we'd probably have better luck convincing them if—" Leeann cocked her head to one side "—say, one of their own had already agreed to participate?"

It was then Dean noticed she was looking right at him. *Oh, hell no.* "Forget it, Leeann. I'm not interested."

"But you are single, right?" Leeann pressed. "You haven't been steadily involved with anyone for a while."

Dean looked at Priscilla and found her watching him as she scratched Daisy, who'd rolled over onto her back, exposing her belly in a display of contented bliss. "Yes— No— Yes, I'm single, and no, I'm not dating—"

"I'm assuming from your shirt you're involved with the camp somehow?" Priscilla asked.

His empty bottle hit the bar top with a thud. "I volunteer at Camp Diamond because we're open to all kids, even those with disabilities. I'm there to handle any physical-therapy issues that might arise."

"Very admirable. Can I also assume you were born and raised in Destiny?"

"Nope. Sea Point, New Jersey." Dean enjoyed the stunned look on her face. "I'm a beach bum who's only lived out in the Wild West for the last few years. Don't even own a Stetson."

"But you're so popular you might as well be a native," Leeann countered. "You're part of the volunteer fire department and I know there must be a couple of single guys there you could persuade to join the cause. Oh, and you could get the Murphy brothers to sign up, too! Devlin's still in London with Tanya, but Liam and Nolan are single."

Knowing he was fighting a losing battle against Leeann's enthusiasm, Dean looked at his best friend for backup, but Bobby's grin told him he was on his own. There had to be a way to get out of this mess, but damned if he could think of one.

Leeann and Bobby had wanted something that would allow the town to support the camp, even though an event this size probably wouldn't bring in the kind of funds Priscilla was used to. Unless, of course, things got out of hand and she turned it into one of her highfalutin parties or, worse, decided she'd had enough of country life and returned to sunny Southern California, leaving Leeann on her own to pull this off.

He felt the weight of three pairs of eyes staring at him—scratch that, two pairs. Miss Lennox now seemed more interested in the contents of her almost-empty glass and playing kissy-face with that rat of hers after moving on from Daisy.

Dean reached behind the bar for another beer. He grabbed two when Bobby signaled he was ready for one, too, and popped both tops before leaving the safety of the bar. He handed one of the bottles to his friend and then walked over to Priscilla.

She finally looked up at him.

He kept his gaze locked with hers and off her mutt, who was up on all four paws, but, thankfully, silent. Leaning down, he gently tapped his beer against her glass. "Looks like you and I will be working together. Salute."

Leeann jumped to her feet with a happy shout, dragging Bobby with her and wrapping him in a hug. Both dogs joined in with a series of quick barks and Bobby announced it was time to fire up the grill for dinner. The only person who hadn't said anything was Priscilla, who stayed seated, staring up at him with wide eyes.

Had she really thought he wouldn't do it?

Priscilla got to her feet then, and while Dean knew the proper thing was to step back and give her some room, he didn't move an inch. Her perfume, a fresh, summery scent he remembered from yesterday, filled his head, and those sexy high heels of hers put her right at eye level. If either of them took a deep breath…

"Thank you. I'm sure you will be—" his gaze stayed on her face as he waited for her to finish "—very helpful."

He dropped his head a fraction of an inch until their noses almost touched. "You can count on it, princess."

Her eyes sparkled with that now-familiar fire. This time he took a step back, ready for another volley, but before she could reply, Leeann left her husband's arms and joined them. "You know, we should take you out to Camp Diamond for a tour. That way you'll understand what it's all about. We could go tomorrow around noon? After Sunday services."

"Thank you." Pricilla sidestepped toward Leeann and away from Dean. "I'd love to see the camp in person."

"You might want to change your shoes first," he added.

She looked back. "Excuse me?"

He gestured toward her feet with his beer. "Spiked heels versus dirt and grass? My money's on Mother Earth."

And there went the familiar uptilt of her chin. "I've run three city blocks in these heels without breaking a sweat, but I'll keep your advice in mind."

He had a comeback to that, but decided to keep it to himself when Leeann again shot him a dirty look.

"Priscilla, would you mind helping me in the kitchen for a few minutes? I need to make a salad and pull some things together. Bobby, the meat is in the fridge behind the bar. Dean, why don't you see if you can get a fire going… without causing any damage?"

The two women headed across the deck toward the double glass doors that led inside. Snack, or Snake—damn, he was sure he was going to screw that up a few more times and probably out loud—and Daisy were right on their heels.

Dean gave a short whistle that made not only the dogs but Priscilla hesitate, but only Daisy stopped and looked back while the rest continued on their way.

"Hey, you stay out here with me," he said. "Like always."

Daisy only offered him a grin and then disappeared through the open doors before Leeann slid it closed again.

"Will wonders never cease?" Bobby's voice came from close by.

"Tell me about it. Man's faithful companion has deserted me."

"No, I'm talking about the auction." His friend retrieved the steaks from behind the bar. "For a minute there I thought you might actually say no."

Dean walked to the oversize stainless-steel grill, lifted the lid and pressed a button. Presto. Fire. "Yeah, right. Then your wife really would have my hide. I was down for the count as soon as Priscilla asked if I was a bachelor."

"You say that word like it's a bad thing."

"I never thought so until today."

Bobby shot him a grin as he joined him. "At least this way you'll end your dating drought. Even if the lady does have to fork over cold, hard cash."

"Very funny."

"And you know, you might have to add a clause on the auction form that states Daisy won't be anywhere around when the actual date happens."

"Boy, you're a regular comedian today, aren't you? Besides, the auction's not for another month." Dean took another draw from his beer. "You really think I'm going to wait that long?"

"If today was an example of your charming ways with the ladies, I'm not surprised at your empty social calendar," Bobby shot back. "What was with the verbal sparring between you and Priscilla?"

Dean sighed, not quite sure how to answer that without telling his friend the whole story. Did it matter? Would it change anything?

"I mean for someone you've only met twice," Bobby continued as he placed the meat on the heated grill, "you seem to really be—"

"Three times."

Bobby paused, the last steak held in midair. "Huh?"

Knowing this would probably lead to his buddy sharing about his own past with Priscilla—something he had no interest in hearing—Dean quickly rattled off what had really happened down at the river and his second run-in with her at the inn. By the time he got to the mix-up over massage appointments and the fact he'd walked in on her wearing nothing but an oversize bath towel, Bobby was grinning.

"Hmm, I bet that was a nice view." Bobby caught his stare. "What? I'm married, not dead. I can appreciate a pretty lady."

"Yeah, I even caught sight of her tattoo, a yellow rosebud right over her heart," Dean said. "Is that her only one or does she have others in more interesting locations?"

This time Bobby's glare was incredulous. "How in the hell would I know?"

Dean realized right away he'd been wrong. Bobby and Priscilla had never been involved, at least not intimately. Not that she wasn't his type. Bobby had surrounded himself with supermodels, actresses and high-society dames during his racing career. Long before the man returned home and found love again with his high-school sweetheart.

"When she told me she was in town to meet a man, I figured—" Dean was feeling stupider by the minute. "And today you said she was an old friend—"

"Yeah, *friend.* An acquaintance, really. Our paths crossed a lot at charity events over the years." Bobby went back to tending the steaks. "My company still supports some of her foundation's causes, but that's it."

"Foundation?"

"She told you she was a philanthropist."

"I thought that was a fancy way of saying she writes a lot of checks."

"She could do that, too, I suppose. Her family owns the International Lennox Hotel chain, but as long as I've known her she's been working for her family's foundation."

Okay, so she was on the level with her charity work, but something was still off. Dean finished off the last of his beer before tossing the empty bottle in the trash. "Yeah, well, either way, she's too rich for my blood."

"Says the man whose last serious girlfriend was a gold digger from the Big Apple who threw him over for a heart surgeon."

A plastic surgeon, but what did it matter? "That was three years ago. I'm over it. And her."

"Yeah, so over her that you haven't had a steady relationship since."

"That's because of Daisy, and who are you anyway? My mother?" Dean grabbed the extra-long fork and stabbed at the closest slab of raw meat. "For your information, I already asked Pricilla out. Last night. She turned me down."

"No wonder she seemed less than thrilled about working with you for the next month." Bobby shrugged. "Well, look at it this way. You won't have to worry about her bidding on you."

Dean kept his mouth shut as he flipped over the steaks. The thing of it was he wouldn't mind if she did.

Chapter Five

He'd laughed at her idea.

Here in the quiet hush of Sunday morning services with only the pastor's soothing voice filling the air, Priscilla could still hear the husky, masculine sound of Dean Zippenella's amusement ringing in her ears.

Then again, why wouldn't he—both he and Bobby, in fact—laugh? She'd had the same reaction when her sister had come up with a similar idea six months ago, though Priscilla liked to think she'd been a bit more restrained in her refusal to entertain such a notion for a foundation-sponsored event.

Of course, Jacqueline's plan had been to auction off rich and famous bachelors, the crème de la crème from the worlds of entertainment, sports and high tech. And that the starting bid for each of these choice specimens would be five thousand dollars each.

Priscilla couldn't imagine the bids at Destiny's bachelor

auction, much less the total profits for the evening, coming anywhere close to that amount.

Bobby and Leeann had made it clear yesterday that making money was secondary to having an event that the whole town could participate in. While Bobby hadn't been on board right away, Leeann's excitement had been genuine and infectious. So much so that Priscilla had found herself agreeing to stay in this slice of Norman Rockwell's America for the next month to help pull it all together.

The last thing she'd admit was that she'd never done an event like this before. But how different could this type of auction be from any other? Of course, the first order of business was to get something—or more precisely, a few someones—for the ladies to bid on.

That was where Dean Zippenella came in.

Leeann had felt the need to apologize for the man's behavior once they were alone in her spacious kitchen, but Priscilla had insisted that none was needed. She'd then gone on to declare her certainty that she and Dean would be able to work together for the good of the auction.

She hoped.

Dinner conversation had been centered on the auction and the camp, with Leeann and Bobby doing most of the talking, while Dean joined in from time to time, in between sneaking bits of his steak to his dog. He also attempted, unsuccessfully, to get Snake to take one of his offerings. The look on his face when her pup turned up his nose at the meat had Priscilla hiding a giggle behind her napkin.

Really, when was the last time she had giggled?

Dean had picked up on it, but the gleam in his eyes told her he was even more determined to get Snake to accept his gift. Which the dog never did, leaving the small cut of steak lying on the deck until Dean finally allowed Daisy to steal the morsel.

After that, the discussion had turned to her work with her family's foundation, but soon the sound of Jerry Lee Lewis's "Great Balls of Fire" had filled the air, cutting her off. Dean had reached for his cell phone while pushing back from the table, only half-finished with his meal, to answer.

Bobby had explained the ringtone meant the call was from the firehouse and as a volunteer firefighter Dean was most likely being called in for duty. When Dean ended the call, he had confirmed Bobby's explanation before thanking his friends for dinner. His gaze had barely strayed in her direction as he said goodbye, which was so different than earlier when he'd stood close and looked intently at her, promising to be…helpful.

Confused, she'd brushed away the feeling as he and Daisy disappeared into the woods to return to the camp, where he'd left his truck.

It'd been after six by the time she got back to the inn, and she'd kept busy the rest of the evening doing extensive research on bachelor-auction fund-raisers. Just to be safe, she'd downloaded her folder for the fine-arts auction held two years ago in Malibu and set about replacing words like *painting* and *sculpture* with *eligible bachelor.*

And she found herself thinking about Dean Zippenella. A lot.

She'd also come across Destiny's website last night, and the history of the town's founding back in the late 1800s was fascinating. Who would've guessed the Painted Lady Inn had once been a brothel? But it was the page devoted to town services, specifically the fire department, that had drawn her attention. One page featured photographs of training exercises and an annual competition of sorts against other fire departments and included images of the men and women in the department. There'd been one of Dean, smiling wide despite a soaking-wet T-shirt plastered to his body and baggy fireman pants, complete with red suspenders that hung loose at his hips. She'd stared at the picture for a long time before copying it to her bachelor-auction file, telling herself it was purely for research, but when she found herself wondering if Dean would be at the camp today for the tour, she quickly closed the file and concentrated instead on writing up her notes about the personal sponsorships for the camp, certain that her fund-raising idea was a sound one.

The pastor's sermon ended and the congregation rose, Priscilla with them, realizing she'd missed most of what the man had said thanks to her daydreaming and shared a quick smile with Minnie Gates, who sat next to her. She'd planned to attend services this morning alone, slipping quietly into the back of the church, but when Minnie and Major Gates had offered to walk with her during breakfast at the inn, she couldn't find a way to gracefully refuse.

When the choir began to sing and chatter filled the church, Priscilla guessed the services were over.

"Would you like to come back with us?" Minnie leaned back into the pew, her husband already standing in the aisle talking with someone as the choir finished singing.

"No, thank you. I think I'll stay here for a moment longer." Priscilla hadn't spotted Bobby or Leeann yet, but she figured it would be easier to find them in the parking lot after the crowd thinned. "But I appreciate you letting me tag along with you and the Major."

"Of course, dear. Now, don't you leave without making a wish, seeing as how this is your first time in our little church."

She promised, though she'd never heard of the tradition before. She waited until the church was almost empty, offering smiles to those who met her gaze, before she closed her eyes, pulled in a deep breath and slowly released it.

A wish, huh? Should she ask for no one in town to recognize her from her recent bout with the tabloids during her stay? How about a phone call from her father where he was more concerned about her feelings over this mess with her sister than with the gossip Jacqueline's actions created?

Hmm, too complicated. Yes, something easier. World peace, perhaps? Or maybe she should ask for something totally unexpected like—

She felt more than heard someone slide into the pew next to her. Looking up, she was surprised to find Dean sitting there. "What are you doing here?"

"The same as you, I'd guess." He kept his voice low, gaze forward, as he folded his hands together in his lap. "Better to beg for forgiveness than ask permission, I always say."

Blaming the sudden warmth flooding her veins on the warm July day and not on the way a freshly shaved Dean looked this morning was easier said than done. He was dressed in a starched white shirt, sleeves rolled back along his forearms, and khakis with a sharply pressed crease down the center of each pant leg. She caught a quick whiff of the man's spicy cologne and had to catch her breath.

She stopped taking inventory long enough to realize they were the only two people left inside the simple country church. "I wasn't doing either."

"Well, there's nothing wrong with a simple prayer or two," Dean said, still not looking at her. "They say He answers every one."

"Do you honestly believe that?"

"Sure." This time he looked at her and she read exhaustion in his dark eyes. "But sometimes the answer is no."

His reply startled her and then she remembered why he'd left so suddenly yesterday. "How did it go with your—with the call you got? I hope everything turned out okay."

Now it was Dean's turn to be surprised. She could see

he hadn't expected her to say that. He blinked and then looked down at his hands. "Not good. There was a two-car crash out on the highway heading toward Laramie. We were called in to handle the resulting brush fire. It took most of the night, but we managed to get it out before too much damage was done to the surrounding acreage."

A deep breath expanded his chest before he slowly released it. He gazed forward again and continued, "Can't say the same for the people. The driver of the car who caused the crash didn't make it. Four teenagers in the other car are in the hospital."

His words tugged at her heart. "Oh, my. Do you know any of them?"

He shook his head. "Nope. Neither car was from Destiny."

Silence filled the air and Priscilla struggled with what to say next, which was so unlike her. She'd always been able to talk to anyone in any given situation. What was it about this man that made her so...uncertain? "Maybe you should have skipped church this morning and slept in instead."

He turned to her with one raised eyebrow. "It's just that you look so tired," she added.

"I am tired. You ready to get out of here?"

Priscilla nodded, assuming Bobby and Leeann would be waiting outside for her.

"Besides, my *nonni* always knows when I skip out on Sunday services," Dean said, getting to his feet and moving into the aisle. "Don't ask me how, since she's firmly entrenched on the Jersey Shore, but she'll text me with a pointed question just the same."

She was impressed his grandmother knew what texting was. Her father had barely figured out his smartphone, but then again, he had a secretary available practically twenty-four hours a day.

Priscilla stood, one hand casually brushing her skirt back into place as she held her clutch purse in the other. She caught Dean's gaze trailing over her from her head to her feet, where it lingered. This morning, she'd chosen a chocolate-brown silk jacquard dress and matching heels, complete with saucy bows on the toes, hoping she wouldn't be too overdressed. Judging from the number of people wearing jeans and simple cotton sundresses—and Dean's apparent fascination with her shoes—she had been.

"I do plan to take your advice," she said, heading for the exit with Dean right beside her as they walked out into the sunshine, "and change my outfit, including my shoes, before visiting the camp today."

"Good to know, seeing as how I've been elected as your tour guide."

His words caused Priscilla to stumble, one foot catching in the concrete grooves at the top of the stairs. She teetered a moment, grabbing for the nearby handrail, but it was Dean's hand, warm and solid at the small of her back, that steadied her.

"Whoa, careful there," he said. "You okay?"

"I'm fine." As fine as she could be with the weight of his hand just inches above her backside creating zingers that careened inside of her body. "What did you just say?"

"Bobby called. It seems Leeann's caught some bug. She's been throwing up since before dawn, so they can't make it today."

"Oh, th-that's terrible." Priscilla started down the church steps, conscious of Dean's touch, which remained in place as his footsteps matched hers. "I hope Leeann is feeling better soon, but you don't have to show me the camp."

"What's the matter, princess? Tired of my company already?"

Priscilla opened her mouth to respond, but the few people still standing around turned to look at them with open interest before calling out hellos to Dean. He waved and returned the greetings, but never let go of her even when they reached the sidewalk. In fact, he moved even closer as a group of people headed their way. She should've felt crowded, usually preferring to maintain her personal space, but instead his actions came across as protective and gentlemanly.

In fact, Priscilla wasn't bothered at all. She liked it.

"Hey, where'd you go? Falling asleep on me?"

Priscilla blinked, Dean's voice cutting off her thoughts. She turned to him. Out here in the bright sun, his exhaustion was ever more pronounced. "You're the one who needs sleep, remember? We can do the tour another day."

He slipped on a pair of dark sunglasses. "I told Bobby I'd do this."

"Did you also tell him what time you got to bed this morning?"

He sighed. "Are you always so argumentative?"

"Are you always so stubborn?"

Before he could reply, they were surrounded by a half-dozen people, including the pastor. Dean turned on the charm and introduced her to everyone. Priscilla again read the curiosity in their gazes, especially when he explained that she was here to coordinate a fund-raiser for the summer camp. When pressed for details, Dean would only smile and say that an announcement would be coming soon, probably at Wednesday night bingo.

"You're a physical therapist who volunteers at a summer camp and the local fire department, *and* you host a weekly bingo night?" Priscilla asked once they were alone again and making their way to the parking lot. "Is there anything you don't do?"

"I don't sleep much." He stopped and looked around. "I don't see your car. You walked here from the inn?"

Priscilla nodded.

"Come on, I'll give you a ride back so you can change." Dean pulled a set of keys from his pocket. "We can go to the camp together."

It only took one look at his oversize pickup truck for her to realize there was no way she could climb into or out of his vehicle and keep her dignity intact. But before she could point that out to him, he'd opened the passenger door and easily lifted her into the seat.

Speechless, Priscilla hurried to right her skirt, noticing how his shaded gaze seemed momentarily glued to her bared legs. Then he stepped back, closed the door and got in behind the wheel. Silence stretched between them and Priscilla was once again at a loss for words to fill the void. Minutes later they pulled into the parking lot at the inn. Dean backed into a shady spot and shut off the engine.

"Hold on." He slid out from behind the wheel and headed around the front of his truck.

Priscilla released the seat belt and opened the door, planning to slip out and land on her feet before he got to her. "I think I can manage."

"I said hold on." He reached for her again, but this time her forward motion had her landing against his chest.

Latching on to his shoulders, she held tight as he eased her down the length of him. A wall of solid muscle against her curves. Her breath caught and she found herself staring at her own wide-eyed reflection in his dark shades, suddenly wishing she'd taken a moment to put on her own glasses.

"Why did you do that?" His words came out in a raspy whisper.

She could feel the ground beneath her feet—at least she thought she could—but he didn't let go of her. "Do what?"

"Grab on to me."

"You told me to hold on." Which was true, but now there was no reason for her to continue to do so. She dropped her hands and he did the same. "Thanks for helping me."

Dean took a step back, stumbling over the purse she'd dropped when she'd latched on to him. He bent and picked it up, taking his time rising to his full height, his gaze once again moving slowly over her. He handed her the purse. "I'll wait out here while you change. You bringing along your little companion?"

Priscilla blinked and pressed her clutch to her chest. Still breathless from all of this close contact, she fought to understand what he was talking about. "Oh, you mean— No, I don't think so. I don't really know anything about the camp and I wouldn't want him to get lost. I had him out for a walk early this morning, so—" She stopped when she realized she was rambling. She never rambled. "I'm sure Snake will be fine in the room."

"Good. I won't have to worry about my shoes, then. Don't take too long, okay? It's lunchtime."

She glanced at her watch, noting he was right. It was half past noon. "I'm sorry, am I getting in the way of your next meal?"

"Nope, because this time you'll be joining me."

Was he asking her out on a date again? "I will?"

"Me and about fifty or so campers." He crossed his arms over his chest and leaned back against his truck. "In the camp's dining hall. If memory serves, on Sundays the menu is mac and cheese, sliders with or without cheese, and apple crisp."

Confusion filled her. "Sliders?"

"Yeah, sliders." Dean cupped his hands. "You know, mini hamburgers? Just the right size for a kid."

So she'd never eaten a mini hamburger before? Big deal. Before she could think about it, she reached for his hands and gave them a quick squeeze. "They sound divine. I won't be but a moment."

She let go and turned away, the prickly feeling on her fingers matching the one between her shoulders that told her Dean was watching her every step. She put a bit more swing into her hips as she walked up onto the inn's covered front porch. Giving in to the urge to confirm her suspicion, she paused and looked back. Yes, he still stood in the same spot, his gaze fixed on her. At least it seemed that way. An unexpected smile creased her lips as she entered the inn and hurried to her room.

Once inside, she leaned back against the door, pressed a hand to her stomach and released a deep breath. What was she doing? One minute the man was putting his hands on her with an ease and familiarity she'd never felt before and now she was flirting with him?

She'd only met Dean Zippenella forty-eight hours ago!

Goodness, up until last week she'd been in a committed—at least on her part—relationship. Her first long-term one since college, as her work kept her very busy. In fact, Jonathan had been the one to pursue her. Relentlessly in the beginning, but once they'd established their relationship, they'd both been so busy with their work and social calendars that they'd settled into…what? Was what she had with her ex so sedate and lackluster that he'd been compelled to find someone else, even if that someone was her sister? Did that explain why she found herself so attracted to—

A subtle beeping came from Priscilla's purse, interrupting her thoughts. She opened it and grabbed her cell phone.

"Hello?" Silence greeted her. She could tell the call was live, but no one responded. "Hello? Is anyone there?"

"Hey, Priscilla."

Jacqueline. Her sister's voice held that breathless quality that always reminded her of an animated cartoon princess, but now it sounded a bit shaky, as well. Still, it was Priscilla's legs that gave out. She sank onto the closest chair. Snake, who hadn't budged from his pillow when she entered the room, scurried to her side and plopped down at her feet, his face a study of doggy concern.

Priscilla opened her mouth, but no sound came out. She checked the screen on the phone just to be sure. Yes, there was the image of her sister's smiling face looking back at her. She'd been so caught up in her thoughts she hadn't bothered to check.

"Priscilla, please. I know you're still there." Jaq's voice was stronger as it came through the speaker. "Please talk to me."

She pressed the phone to her ear while bending over to give Snake a quick scratch behind his ears. "I have nothing to say to you."

"But you answered my call. I was so sure you wouldn't."

"If I'd been smart enough to check the display first, you'd be speaking to my voice mail now." Priscilla's words snapped off her tongue as a thread of anger finally overcame her shock. She jumped to her feet and paced the length of the room. "Especially since this is the first time you've called since—since last Wednesday."

"I didn't think you'd want to hear from me."

She hadn't. She wasn't ready to deal with her sister. After she returned Jonathan's ring, something she planned to have her assistant take care of as soon as she returned home, their three-year relationship would be officially over.

Not that there was any doubt now, but repairing things with Jacqueline… "You were right."

"Oh, Sissy…"

The use of the childhood nickname caused Priscilla's heart to squeeze in her chest. As a toddler, Jacqueline had trouble pronouncing her name, so she'd often called her "sister," which had soon turned into Sissy, a name that stuck to this day, especially when the two of them were having a private talk.

Or when Jacqueline wanted to wheedle her way out of another mess.

"Look, I'm a little busy at the moment—"

"It just happened. We didn't plan… We didn't want to hurt you." Her sister's rushed words filled her ear. "There was never any attraction between Jonathan and me until that night. I mean, yes, I've always thought he was a hottie, and I sometimes teased you about wanting him for myself, but I didn't mean anything by it. It's just that we were both standing there on the red carpet, each of us alone, so we just sort of turned to each other. We connected, and that's when the camera flashes started going off…."

Priscilla's thoughts raced back to that night. She'd been standing backstage in front of a monitor that showed the steady stream of celebrity arrivals, including Jonathan, who must've just received her note that she wouldn't be joining him out front as previously planned. He hadn't been happy about being stood up—she could see that from his facial expression—but then moments later, Jacqueline appeared at his side, looking amazing in a rhinestone-and-tulle getup.

She remembered the surprise on Jonathan's face, but then it shifted to something else as he tightened his arm around Jacqueline's waist and flashed his perfect smile at her and the cameras.

"Well, I guess I should be thankful that your betrayal

was so spur-of-the-moment and hadn't been going on behind my back for the last three years." Priscilla stopped her pacing and grabbed at the back of the desk chair, needing something solid to hold on to.

"Priscilla—"

"I can't talk about this now, Jaqueline." Her gaze fell to the paperwork concerning the auction and the camp spread out over her desk. "I need to get back to work."

"But Dad said you'd taken off for your extended vacation."

Surprised filled her. "You've spoken to him?"

"Ah, well, no…actually, it was Elizabeth who took my call. Dad was busy. As usual. And probably still too pissed to talk to me."

Yes, Priscilla was sure her sister was right on both counts.

"Where are you?" Jacqueline continued. "You didn't go to France, did you?"

The question confused her for a moment. Then she realized where her sister and her ex had disappeared to. And why she was suddenly calling her. "Are you worried we might bump into each other along Boulevard de la Croisette?"

"No, of course not! I mean, yes, I suppose—and it might be awkward—"

"Might be?" That was it. She was done with this conversation. "Well, don't concern yourself. I am about as far away from France as I could be, and you know what? I'm beginning to believe that's a good thing. A very good thing."

"Priscilla, do you really think you should have left town? I know you had plans, but I'm sure Daddy and the foundation want you back where you can…you know, take care of things. Important things."

"Do not tell me what I should or shouldn't be doing. You're the one who caused this mess and I'm not going to fix—" Priscilla pressed a hand to her lips, cutting off her own words. No. She wasn't going to advise her sister on what needed to be done. Not this time. Not about this. "I'm hanging up now."

"Wait! When can I talk to you again?"

"I honestly don't know." The tightness in her chest doubled, making it hard for Priscilla to breathe. "Goodbye, Jacqueline."

Lowering the phone, she could still hear her sister's voice, but a quick press of the button and it was gone. She sank into the chair. Snake hurried to her side, leaned against her legs and sighed. Seconds later, the phone lay forgotten on the desk as she held the soothing warmth of the tiny dog to her chest, his wet nose snuggled against her neck.

"Thank you for the loving, Snake, but I can't sit here and get lost in this crazy mess. I have someone waiting for me and he's probably not happy that I'm making him late for lunch."

Priscilla lowered the pup back to the floor and then quickly stripped out of her dress and heels, trying to keep her sister's last words out of her head. And failing. Who did Jacqueline think she was handing out advice on what she should be doing?

"You *shouldn't* have cheated with your sister's boyfriend." Priscilla eyed the outfit laid out on her bed, knowing it wasn't exactly the best for hiking in the forest, but it was all she had to work with for now. "Even if that sister's broken heart isn't anywhere near as shattered as she'd thought it'd be. Especially with a very handsome firefighter waiting for her downstairs."

Thinking about Dean had her pausing after she dressed. She looked at herself in the bathroom mirror. What would he think of her simple outfit, complete with ballerina flats, the only low-heeled shoes she had with her?

And why did she care?

Realizing the formal French twist she'd put her hair up in for church was too much for her afternoon plans, she quickly removed the pins and instead pulled it back in a casual ponytail. She gave herself a quick spritz of perfume and was halfway through reapplying her lipstick when she caught herself.

"It's what you do every time you freshen up," she spoke to her reflection, "no matter who is waiting for you."

She then turned away, grabbing her leather tote with her trusty portfolio inside, gave Snake a quick belly rub and left.

Back outside, she'd expected Dean to still be standing by his truck, but he was sitting behind the wheel. She opened the door and his head snapped up from where it'd been resting against the seat cushions. "Hey, let me help—"

"No need."

"But your skirt—"

"It's not a skirt." She grabbed the bar on the doorframe and hauled herself into the truck. "It's a skort."

Dean yanked his sunglasses off his face. "What the hell is a skort?"

"One part skirt, one part shorts." Closing the door, she placed her bag at her feet and fastened her seat belt. "Okay, let's go."

He stared at her for a moment, then started the engine, put his glasses back on and pulled out onto the street.

Priscilla kept her gaze either firmly in front of her or out the passenger-side window as they left town, taking the same road that led to Bobby and Leeann's place. The businesses and homes of Destiny gave way to lush green forest as they drove, but all Priscilla could see was the sunny beaches and resort towns of the Mediterranean coastline in the southeast corner of France.

"Are you telling me you didn't pack a single pair of jeans in those half-dozen suitcases I saw in the back of your car?" Dean asked, breaking into her thoughts. "And some sneakers?"

"It was only four suitcases." And her garment bag. And her makeup tote, but that wasn't technically a suitcase. Besides, when was the last time she'd actually worn jeans? College? Priscilla couldn't remember. "When I packed for this trip, the plan was to spend the rest of the summer at… at a friend's château in the South of France, not out here in cowboy country."

Dean's fingers tightened on the steering wheel but he remained silent. They passed the long driveway that lead to Bobby and Leeann's house and continued for a few minutes before taking a turn beneath a wooden arch emblazoned with the camp's name. Dean drove past a parking lot, following a winding road that led deeper into the forest. Soon, they came to a clearing with a view of a beautiful lake and numerous log buildings scattered among the trees.

He pulled to a stop next to one of the buildings and shut off his truck. "And when your plans changed, you didn't switch out your wardrobe before you hit the road?" he asked.

"The only thing I was thinking about hitting at the time was my ex-boyfriend, squarely on the jaw." Shocked at her own words, Priscilla released the latch on her seat belt, wanting nothing more than to be out of this truck.

This was a bad idea. She should've just gone back down to the parking lot and told Dean she couldn't do the tour. But they were here, so she might as well get it over with. She grabbed her tote and reached for the door handle.

"Wait a minute," Dean called out. "You wanted to take a swing at your boyfriend? Why?"

"My *ex*-boyfriend," Priscilla emphasized, "when I found him getting all hot and heavy with my sister!"

"Your sister?" Dean's voice was incredulous, but then it switched to concern. "Hey, watch out. Those pine needles can be a bit—"

The moment she jerked free of the truck and her feet hit the ground, they disappeared out from under her. Seconds later, Priscilla found herself flat on her back on a cushion of pine needles and grass. Stunned but not hurt, she blinked, staring up at the towering trees and the bright blue sky. Closing her eyes, she covered them with one hand, willing back the tears that threatened to escape.

She didn't cry. Ever. Not since her mother's funeral all those years ago. Not after her father told her that tears were a sign of weakness and Lennox women were never weak. Not even when she'd found her sister with…

As the first drop freed itself from the corner of her eye, warm fingers touched her shoulder, then moved up to whisk away the offending moisture. When she opened her eyes, she found Dean kneeling beside her. And the look on his face was the last thing she wanted to see: pity. Oodles of it. Directed right at her.

Chapter Six

"Are you okay?" Dean gazed down at her, glad to see her blue eyes clear and focused as she stared back at him. And free from more tears. Other than the one clinging to his fingertips. "Does anything— Does it hurt anywhere?"

She closed her eyes again. "I don't want to talk about it."

Yeah, with news like she'd spouted a minute ago, he wasn't surprised. News that had brought her to tears.

"I meant physically," he said. "Does any part—your back, your legs—hurt?"

She pulled in a deep breath and released it, shaking her head. "The only thing bruised right now is my pride."

"These pine needles can be slick, even in the best of shoes." He looked her over with a professional eye, making sure she wasn't injured. "Which those things on your feet definitely aren't."

"Yes, I'm aware of that fact." Priscilla's eyes snapped open and she started to sit up. "Painfully aware."

Unlike the first time down at the river, Dean didn't ask if she needed help. He just took one of her hands in his and, wrapping his arm around her back, rose with her when she got to her feet.

So far, so good. She didn't seem to mind his assistance, then or now. "You sure you're okay?"

Priscilla kept her gaze to the ground, brushing pine needles and dirt from her clothes, righting the neckline of her silky top, which had slipped off one shoulder. "I'm fine. Where's my purse?"

Dean spotted the bag lying nearby, but before he could move, Priscilla saw it. She leaned down, grabbing for the straps, and her feet once again fought for purchase on the needle-strewn ground. Before he could help her, she stuck out one hip and found her balance. "Dammit, I'm normally not such a klutz!"

She whipped around, eyes wide, fingers pressed hard against her mouth.

"What?" Dean instinctively reached for her again. "What's wrong?"

"I'm sorry." Dropping her hand, she squared her shoulders and pulled in a deep breath. She tucked her bag up on her shoulder, releasing a whispery sigh as she did. "Please forgive my swearing. It's something I rarely do."

Dean grinned. "Don't worry about it. I swear all the time. Usually in my head and in Italian, but a few choice phrases have slipped free now and then. You're only human, right?"

Priscilla nodded and offered a faint smile. He noticed she still had a few pine needles in her hair. He took a step closer and pulled them free, ignoring the startled expression on her face. "You missed some."

"Oh, I must look a mess." She took a step back, her fingers running through the long lengths.

"You look fine." Better than fine. A bit messy and sexy, but he managed to keep that observation to himself. He lifted his sunglasses from the top of his head and put them back in place over his eyes. "A little overdressed for a kids' camp, but—"

"What about you?" She cut him off. "Do you always come out here in pressed khakis and a button-down shirt?"

Dean looked down. Yeah, he'd forgotten he was still in his Sunday best. "You're right, but I can easily fix that." He released the top three buttons on his shirt and then started pulling the bottom edge from the waistband of his pants.

"Wait!" Priscilla cried out. "What are you doing?"

"Getting more comfortable. Just give me a second." He reached back between his shoulder blades and, with one tug, pulled his shirt easily over his head. He wore a simple white T-shirt underneath, and seeing as how the day was already warm, he did feel more relaxed. Tossing his dress shirt inside the truck, he turned to Priscilla. "Much better. Ready to tackle the chow hall?"

She stared at him, mouth agape, then snapped it closed and nodded instead.

Dean found he liked the idea of rendering her speechless. "Just take it slow and steady, okay?"

"Are you worried I might not make it there in one piece?"

He stepped to one side and directed her to walk ahead of him. "I'll walk a few paces behind to catch you if you fall, princess."

Her chin now held that familiar upward tilt as she walked past. "I'm sure that won't be necessary. And the name is Priscilla."

Despite what he'd just said, Dean walked next to her, pointing at the largest of the log buildings ahead as they moved into the bright sunshine. The camp was quiet, except for the noisy chatter filtering from the open windows of the dining hall. "I know what your name is."

"Surely if I can pronounce Zippenella, you can handle my name. Or would Ms. Lennox be easier for you?"

And the hoity-toity princess was back. Not surprising. The comment she'd made about her finding her sister doing the nasty with her ex still hung in the air. Most people probably wouldn't let something that juicy go without asking for more details, and even though he *was* curious, Dean had seen the shock on her face—and the tears—when she let that news slip out. She probably expected him to ask her about it. He figured it had to be a recent event, since she'd admitted her travel plans had changed so suddenly.

Plans that hadn't included her spending any length of time here in cowboy country. He'd let that little jab at his adopted hometown slide, only because he could tell from the moment she returned from changing her clothes something had been bothering her.

Boy, was it ever. The thing of it was, Dean could appreciate what she was going through.

Being the second oldest of six kids, he knew quite a bit about the good, the bad and the ugly of sibling relationships. Hell, just a few years before he'd moved to Destiny, Dean had come across his brother making out in the family's backyard gazebo with a girl Dean had brought to the house for a family dinner. Granted, they'd only been dating a few weeks, and according to a few not-so-subtle hints from his siblings, the girl had been all wrong for him. Still, the betrayal had caused a rift that started with Dean's right hook to Frankie's jaw and lasted for a few weeks until his brother found out the girl had been using both him and Dean to make an old boyfriend jealous.

Of course, Frankie had tried to tell Dean his tastes hadn't improved when he'd started dating Kate shortly after that, but Dean hadn't listened then, either. Thankfully, he didn't have to witness her betrayal firsthand, but after being together for almost a year, it'd been a blow all the same to find out about her trying to use his old man's position as police chief to her advantage to make a few—quite a few—parking tickets in their beach community go away. Learning about her engagement to another man via a front-page article in the style section of the *New York Times* a week later had been the icing on a very bitter cake.

Yeah, Katherine Bartlett Barrington had never intended to get serious with him. She'd been slumming far from her ritzy Manhattan neighborhood when they'd met. Bored and looking for something—or someone—to take the shine off her high-society world for a while, she'd gone fishing and he'd taken the bait.

Something Ms. Lennox and his ex-girlfriend had in common, maybe?

"Ms. Lennox might be easier, but not as much fun," Dean finally answered as they walked up the wide steps. He yanked open the screen door and allowed Priscilla to enter the center hallway of the building ahead of him. "On the left are the camp offices and farther down is the store where campers and staff can get everything from T-shirts to toothpaste. On the right is the dining hall, and as you can probably tell from the noise level, lunch has been served."

Priscilla stopped outside the closest set of double doors, her eyes wide as she took in the controlled chaos through the clear plastic windows. "How many children are in there?"

"About fifty or so, and the staff." Dean pocketed his sunglasses and then grabbed the door handle. "Come on, let's eat."

He led her into the melee, a bit surprised when she inched closer to him. He put his hand at the small of her back, giving a quick tour of the place, pointing out the busy kitchen area off to one side and the rows of tables and benches filled with campers and staff that stretched out in front of them.

"All of the meals are served family-style and the campers pull mess-hall duties—dishing out the food, cleaning up afterward—during their stay. Of course, besides the daily menu, the kids can go à la carte if they want." Dean led her to a corner nook separated from the main dining space by a long counter that held the drink machines, trays and silverware. He waved a hand at the expansive salad-bar area, complete with plenty of fresh fruit, pasta and potato salads, and two different soups. "Because as you know, not everyone likes burgers. See anything that interests you?"

Priscilla turned to look at him and he'd swear that her gaze shifted to his mouth. And it stayed there. A hunger to lean in and cover those soft, shiny pink lips with his own crashed into him with a force he hadn't felt in a long time. If ever. Dean could readily admit he'd been attracted to Priscilla from the moment they'd met, even if it was clear she was out of his league. But that realization didn't quench the desire to pull her into his arms and kiss her, right here in front of everyone.

Did she feel the same way? A light flush danced over her cheeks, and this time when she lifted her chin, her gaze moved to his and he read the answering desire in those blue depths. She wanted this as much as he did. Was she as surprised as he was?

Just then the crash of dropped dishes from the other side of the room brought forth shrieks, laughter and loud applause, breaking the moment and bringing both of them back to reality.

Priscilla looked away first. "Uh, no, thank you. There's nothing here...I'm interested in."

Dean reached out, snagging a cherry-red miniature tomato and popping it into his suddenly dry mouth. "Why, Ms. Lennox, I think you just told a great big fib."

"And of course I apologized profusely, but I have to admit it was hard to do so with a straight face."

Priscilla sat on a stone bench in a small garden nestled between the white clapboard church and the attached hall, enjoying the light breeze on a still-warm summer evening. It'd been a week ago tonight that her world turned upside down, but she now felt so far removed from her old life in Beverly Hills that despite that unfortunate phone call with her sister, it seemed as if everything that happened last Wednesday had happened to someone else.

Priscilla had received an email from her best friend begging for an update on her adventures in Destiny and had decided to call back despite only having a few minutes to talk. She was here at the town's weekly bingo night to meet up with Leeann and Bobby and to share the news about the auction. She'd already told Lisa about the awful phone call with her sister, the beautiful inn she was staying at and how she'd agreed to organize the fund-raiser she'd come up with off the top of her head.

"Oh, Lisa, the sight of him soaking wet from the knees down and the *squish-squish-squish* coming from his shoes with every step was too funny."

"Well, at least you didn't completely capsize the canoe when you tried for your less-than-graceful exit," Lisa said.

"His first clue that we were going to have trouble should've been the fact I kept losing the paddle in the water. I tried to tell him I'd never been in a canoe before, but he insisted that I go."

"And he paid the price for it." Lisa's rich laughter filled the air. "But I like the part about how you almost knocked him down earlier in the tour thanks to the creepy crawler in the girls' shower room."

"Hey, that spider was big and brown and hairy and yuck!" Priscilla shuddered at the memory of poking her head inside one of the individual shower stalls and coming nose to nose with the offensive creature. "I just wanted to get away from the thing. Dean happened to be standing between me and the only exit."

"Boy, you and this Zipperman seem to spend all your time falling for each other."

"I am not falling for Dean *Zippenella,* even if I do seem to end up on my backside more often than not when he's around." Something she'd managed to avoid for the remainder of the camp tour, the spider incident notwithstanding.

"It also sounds like you've really taken to the camp," Lisa said. "Considering English riding is the closest thing you've ever done connected with the great outdoors."

Lisa was right. The grounds had been impressive: the outdoor sports area had open fields for baseball and soccer as well as a basketball court and an archery range. The challenge course, with the ropes and cables and platforms some twenty or so feet off the ground, looked a bit intimidating, but Dean assured her proper safety measures were in place for both the campers and the staff. All the swimming and boating activities were held at the lake, and the campfire circle sported plenty of seating around a large fire pit.

The health center housed an infirmary and sleeping quarters for the full-time nurse and for any ill campers that needed to stay there, while the cabins and bathhouses for the girls and boys, separated by a dense patch of trees, were bright and airy. Similarly, the arts-and-crafts building had plenty of light and lots of room for budding artists of all kinds.

"And we never even made it down to the stables that

first day." Priscilla crossed her legs and eyed her high heels. They felt a bit strange on her feet, as this was the first time she'd wore them this week. "But I have been back at the camp every afternoon—with Snake in tow, of course—and the horses they have for the kids are great."

"I hope you've done some shoe shopping while you've been there. Your Louboutins must be taking a beating with all that grass and dirt."

"Would you be surprised to find out I've been wearing nothing but jeans, T-shirts and the cutest pair of outdoor hiking boots for the last three days?"

"What?" Shock filled Lisa's voice. "This from the girl who has nothing made of denim in her entire closet? Oh, you must send me a picture."

Priscilla looked down at her lap. "Well, at the moment I'm back to wearing a dress and heels. I'm about to formally announce the auction."

"At what? A town meeting?"

"Actually, it's the weekly bingo night at the local church hall." Priscilla looked at the crowd filing into the building. She hadn't seen Leeann arrive yet. Or Dean. In fact, she hadn't see Dean since Sunday when he'd dropped her off back at the inn. Though Leeann had shared with her earlier today that they'd secured some bachelors for the event, Priscilla wasn't sure if Dean had anything to do with that or not.

Just then her gaze caught on the tall figure walking across the parking lot. Dressed casually in jeans and T-shirt, Dean headed toward a red convertible pulling into a parking space a few feet from hers. While she loved her new Mercedes with a passion, the other convertible was obviously a vintage model and a very beautiful one at that. Bobby and Leeann got out of the car and joined Dean, heading for the hall.

It only took a moment before they passed her car. As they did, Dean slowed and reached out, his fingertips seeming to gently caress the trunk. A shiver raced through Priscilla as if the man had just touched her skin.

"So tell me more about this bachelor auction. Which is a simply yummy idea!" Her friend's voice broke into her thoughts. "Sugar, I am so tempted to fly out there and bid on a cowboy for myself. Or a firefighter. Unless I'd be stepping on someone's toes?"

Priscilla shot to her feet, reaching back for her leather tote. "I have no idea what you're talking about."

Lisa laughed again. "Oh, listen to my best friend all flustered!"

"I have to go." After a deep breath—okay, a few deep breaths—she'd be fine. "Things are about to get started."

"If you ask me, they already have! And hey, send me some pictures. I want to see you in cutoff jeans with that hunky firefighter of yours!"

"Dean is not mine. My goodness, this time last week I was wearing another man's ring."

"On your right hand after he gave it to you at the end of a business meeting with a let's-see-where-this-might-be-going speech. Please! We both know you settled for the jerk because he was appropriate and easy and cut from the same expensive cloth as you. Something tells me your Dean is 100 percent the opposite. And that's a good thing."

"I just told you—"

"Oh, I've got to run! Toodles, darling!"

Priscilla wanted to protest further, but her friend had already hung up. She tossed her phone inside her tote, turned her back to the parking lot and inhaled deeply through her nose, the sweet scent of the nearby yellow rose bushes filling her senses. As hard as she tried to rid her head of her friend's parting words with each exhale, Priscilla couldn't help but compare the two men. Other than both being very good-looking, they had nothing in common.

Jonathan was rich, entitled and often so involved with his work it was hard for him to acknowledge anyone else's time or efforts. Dean, on the other hand, seemed to have just as busy of a life, but from his job at the veterans' center to his volunteering with the local fire department and the summer camp, his work was centered on other people's wants and needs.

Including hers?

What did she want? Need? Wasn't that what she was supposed to discover during this time away from Beverly Hills and the foundation?

"And in conclusion, we are very excited to announce the auction will take place three weeks from this coming Friday at the Blue Creek Saloon. We've already secured several bachelors who are excited to participate in this worthwhile event." Priscilla paused and glanced at Dean, who stood nearby, in time to see the slight grimace cross his face. She widened her smile and turned back to the packed room. "We hope you ladies plan to attend, and if any of you bachelors out there would like to join us, please let either Dean or myself know."

"Give us some more names, sweetie!" The loud demand came from a woman who had to use her walker in order to be able to stand up. "Zip is a hell of a catch, but we want to know all our options. Or is that a secret?"

Priscilla hesitated as laughter filled the air. When she'd first started her presentation, it was difficult to judge if she had anyone's attention. Many in the crowd seemed more interested in getting their supplies for the evening or lining up for food and drinks while she spoke about the camp, the hard work Bobby and Leeann had put into the facility over the past year, and all the good things a place like that did for children.

Then Dean had stepped forward to announce the fund-raiser would be a bachelor auction and that he'd been the first one to sign up. He'd taken some good-natured teasing from the crowd, but soon charmed everyone into listening. Priscilla had then stepped back in and kept her remarks short and sweet.

Leeann came forward and laid a hand on Priscilla's arm, giving her a quick squeeze. "We don't want to make any official announcement until we have secured all the gentlemen, but I will tell you that besides Dean, we've got three cowboys, two police officers and three local businessmen up for bid, so stay tuned!"

Cheers and whistles came from everywhere. Dean took that moment to gently remove the microphone from Priscilla's hand. "So I'm not the only prize. Good to know."

"Oh, we wouldn't leave you hanging out there all by your lonesome," Leeann said with a big smile as Bobby joined them. "Now, let's play some bingo!"

"I've got us seats at Elise Murphy's table. You still feeling up to staying?" Bobby asked, putting an arm around his wife.

"Yes, I feel fine. I think I've finally kicked that flu bug."

"But you're still going to the doctor's tomorrow as planned."

Bobby and Leeann kept talking as they walked away while Dean told the crowd the night's events would be starting in just a few minutes. The noise level rose even higher after that and Priscilla wasn't sure where she should go now that her work here was done. Then she saw Leeann waving at her from a table a few rows back.

"You're sticking around, right?"

She turned and found Dean standing behind her. "So it seems. I haven't played in years, but I'm guessing it'll come back to me."

"It's bingo. It's not that hard. Bobby said you've been at the camp every afternoon helping out." His gaze drifted for a moment to her feet. The corner of his mouth rose into a smile. "Hope you've found other shoes to wear."

"As a matter of fact, Leeann took me to a few shops here in town on Monday. I've been properly outfitted."

"I'll bet."

Priscilla had no idea what he meant by that, but before she could ask, they were joined by three men all dressed in the same blue shirt sporting an embroidered emblem for the Destiny Fire Department over their hearts.

"Hey, is this where we sign up for the auction?" the first man asked. Well over six feet tall with dark square-framed glasses, a full mustache and the most mischievous grin Priscilla had ever seen, he wrapped one arm around Dean's shoulders. "Lord knows we can't have Zip here be the sole representative of the department."

Dean sighed. "Like any lady would be crazy enough to bid on you, Hall?"

"Hey, we're all fine examples of the lesser sex. Why not us?"

Dean waved a hand between the men and Priscilla. "Chris Hall, Steve McIntyre, Scott Wallace…this is Priscilla Lennox. Priscilla, these guys are a few of my crew from the firehouse."

Priscilla smiled as she shook hands with each of them, mentally adding their names to the auction list. "It's so nice to meet you all. And thank you for volunteering to be part of the auction. The more the merrier."

"It sounds like this fund-raising stuff is right up your alley," Steve said, "but please don't tell us you're all work and no play."

Confusion filled her. "I'm sorry?"

Dean shrugged off his friend's arm, his smile gone. "Knock it off, Mac."

"Hey, she can bid on a bachelor just like any of the other ladies in the audience, right?"

"Yes, I suppose I could." Now she understood what he meant and the gleam in his eyes told her just who he'd like her to bid on. "But I'll most likely be too busy running things backstage to have the opportunity to participate."

"You sure?" Scott added. "I've got a cabin on a lake outside of town and a sweet eighteen-foot speedboat. We could make it a day on the water."

"Don't listen to him." Chris nudged his friend in the side with his elbow. "I can whip up a gourmet meal that would put a five-star restaurant to shame. Beef bourguignonne with a fine Burgundy wine. After that I'll give you a sunset tour of the countryside on the back of my Harley. How does that sound?"

It sounded wonderful, but not for the reason either of the men suspected. "I think both of those dates sound terrific!"

"You do?" All four male voices spoke in unison.

"What exactly does that mean?" Dean pushed. "You're planning to bid on them?"

"I think any of the ladies would be excited to bid if the bachelors come up with unique date packages." The idea swirled inside her head, quickly taking shape as she spoke. "We could work with some of the local businesses to either donate items or offer services at a discount. This way the lucky lady will know right from the start what kind of date her bachelor will be providing. Doesn't that sound great?"

"What if the guy's plans are for just a simple dinner at one of the local restaurants?" Dean asked.

Priscilla wondered if that was all Dean would plan for his date. "There's nothing wrong with that, of course, but this is a special event and the dates should be, as well. I'm sure we can help those bachelors who need assistance in coming up with ideas. If, say, you were looking for something more creative—"

"Oh, don't worry about me, darling." Dean took a step forward, putting himself directly between her and his buddies. "This bachelor can be as creative as the next guy."

The gleam in his dark eyes as he looked down at her had Priscilla taking him at his word and wondering just how inventive he could be.

Chapter Seven

A week had gone by and Dean still hadn't decided what he was going to do for his bachelor-auction date. He wanted to plan something that would knock Priscilla's socks off, but kept coming up blank whenever he tried to think about it. Besides, how could he decide what to do when he didn't know if his bidder would be using a walker—which would rule out a romantic nighttime hike—or a college kid who never removed her earbuds?

He pulled his truck to a stop in his usual spot at Camp Diamond. Granted, today was the first time he'd really thought about the auction—ah, hell, that wasn't true. Priscilla had been on his mind a lot, both during his waking hours and making a couple of appearances in his dreams at night.

Still, he was coming up empty with any ideas for a night's entertainment with whoever might win him. He'd heard Priscilla's date-package idea had been popular with both the ladies on the auction committee and the guys who'd agreed to participate. They were up to fifteen bachelors and Priscilla wanted each of the dates to be unique. Besides what his firefighting crew had conjured up, the ones most popular with the committee were a sunrise horseback ride with a breakfast picnic, a limo ride to Cheyenne for dinner, and a show and a trip to Jackson Hole for the day via private helicopter.

That last idea had to be Liam Murphy's. Both he and his older brother Nolan had been wrangled into participating in the auction, but as president of Murphy Mountain Log Homes, Liam could afford such a luxury. Especially since the helicopter was part of the family business and Liam himself would be at the controls.

He bet the princess would be interested in bidding on that!

He thought back to how he hadn't spotted Priscilla's little red car in the camp's parking lot out near the main entrance. Since she'd been so gung ho to help out last week, he'd figured she'd be here today. They hadn't seen each other since bingo night, and even then she'd left when Bobby and Leeann did while he'd still been acting as host and calling numbers. The plan had been for the four of them to get together at Bobby's place last Friday for dinner and to discuss the auction, but it had never happened. One emergency after another at the veterans' center had kept him from attending as well as making him miss his physical-therapy session with the Major earlier that same day.

Shutting off the engine, Dean sat in the quiet interior of his truck. Leaning his head back, he pulled in a deep breath and willed his muscles to relax. It never stopped amazing him how many of the young men and women—some of them barely out of their teens—were in need of care after returning home from the ongoing war in the

Middle East. For both their physical and emotional injuries. His caseload held some difficult patients, none more so than an amputee who was still in the beginning stages of learning to live with his new artificial legs after losing his from above the knee when his tank had been bombed. Last Friday the young man had learned his wife had left him for someone else.

Determined to shake off his gloom, Dean got out of the truck and stretched, still tired even though it was well into the afternoon. He'd finally returned home around dawn, and while it felt good to be back in his own bed, it hadn't been the same without Daisy curled up at his feet. She'd been staying with Bobby and Leeann after he'd called and explained what was happening at work. When he and Bobby had spoken earlier today, before Dean headed to the inn to give the Major his therapy session, Bobby had said he'd been bringing Daisy to the camp and they would meet up with him out here.

Daisy had been a regular at Camp Diamond during the building stages last summer and Dean had brought her with him a few times once they opened this year. Given her advanced age, Daisy usually spent her time curled up on a cot next to Dean's desk in the health center, but when she did venture out, she was very friendly with the boys and male staff and avoided getting anywhere near the females.

That was, until she'd met Priscilla.

According to Bobby, Daisy had been the woman's constant companion whenever she was at the house, which had been daily as they worked out the details for the auction.

The auction. Jeez, he really needed to come up with something—

Dean heard a door to the dining hall slam and then a quick bark. He turned, smiling, as a blur of golden-brown fur raced toward him. "Hey, girl!" Kneeling, he welcomed his dog's enthusiastic greeting as Daisy launched into his arms. "Yes, I'm happy to see you, too."

He scratched her behind her ears and accepted lots of doggy kisses, finally rising when Bobby joined them. His friend had a grin on his face and Dean suddenly remembered the other news Bobby had shared when they spoke earlier.

"Congrats, Daddy." He stuck out his hand. "I'm guessing you're going to be sporting a goofy grin until the rug rat arrives sometime around…when?"

"The New Year." Bobby laughed, a look of pure joy on his face as he returned Dean's handshake. "And you bet I am."

Bobby and Leeann had been trying for a baby since they'd married on New Year's Eve a few years ago. His buddy had confided his concerns that his racing accident might be the cause of their inability to conceive, but tests had proven otherwise. The doctors' advice had been to relax and keep trying and it worked.

Dean was genuinely happy for them. "So, does that make me an honorary uncle?"

"Uncle? Hell, Lee and I want you to be our child's godparent."

Stunned, Dean could only stare at his best friend. He and Bobby had met many years ago while serving in the army overseas. Their friendship had been born in the blood, sweat and tears of hellish duty long before the current conflict that was still going on over there. They'd stayed in touch after leaving the army, back before the attacks on the World Trade Center. When Bobby had needed Dean's services as a physical therapist after his crash, Dean had quit his job and followed his buddy to Destiny.

Thanks to his two married sisters, Dean had four nieces and nephews back in New Jersey, but so far hadn't been asked to take on the title of godparent. He was humbled. "Wow, I don't know what to say."

Bobby's grip tightened. "Say yes."

"You sure you want me having such influence over your baby?" Dean tried to go for humor as the responsibilities that went along with the position filled his head. "There's no telling what kind of trouble I could lead them into."

"Your job will be to keep him—or her—out of trouble." Bobby let go of his hand and gave him a hearty thump on the back. "And give good advice, like always listening to their parents, obeying the rules."

"Aw, what's the fun in that?" He smiled, suddenly feeling a lot better than he had just a few moments ago. "I'd be honored. Thanks for asking."

Bobby returned his grin, then turned to stand next to him as they looked out over the camp. "Boy, it sure is quiet around here with the kids gone."

Dean took in the view from this spot, loving how he could see all the way down to the lake and then the stables just off to the right. "Yeah, I'm sorry I missed the bonfire Saturday night."

"The kids missed having you there, too, not to mention your ghost stories."

"Have you guys been working on anything new while I was gone?" Dean asked.

"Yes, we have, and you're here just in time to help." Bobby pointed straight ahead. "See that area staked out across from the arts-and-crafts building?"

Dean spotted the patch of land cordoned off by ropes tethered to a series of evenly spaced stakes. "What's going in there?"

"A performance pavilion."

He looked at his friend. "A what?"

"An outdoor stage. Nolan was here on Wednesday to discuss the design and dimensions. Since Murphy Mountain Log Homes built the original camp buildings, we want any new ones to match. We decided to go with a three-sided structure, with a roof of course, and leave the area in front for seating, probably with the same type of benches we have at the campfire. You want to go down and check it out?"

"Sure." Dean walked next to Bobby while Daisy tagged along, trotting between them. "Is a stage really something the camp needs?"

"Well, we use either the dining hall or the campfire area whenever we do anything like a talent show or the skits the counselors come up with, but this way we'll have a set location for those things. We won't have to shuffle things around as much. It was one of Priscilla's ideas."

Just hearing her name had Dean scanning the camp again, looking for any sign of her. Nothing. Maybe she was inside the office. Or maybe she'd grown tired of the place after a week. Hanging around a kids' camp was a far cry from the European holiday she'd originally planned. She'd claimed at bingo she'd bought more casual clothes, but that night she'd looked just like she always had.

Rich and beautiful and way out of his league.

"The plan is to clear the area for the foundation. We want to get it poured tomorrow." Bobby's voice droned on until he finally nudged Dean and said, "Hey, did you hear what I just said?"

"No, I was thinking—what did you say?"

"I said I volunteered you to help the crew get the foundation in place." Bobby grinned. "But I think the only thing you heard was that the idea came from Priscilla."

His friend was right about that. "Why does she figure the camp needs an outdoor stage?"

"The kids held an unplanned talent show after lunch on Friday. I wasn't there to see it, but I guess Priscilla was a good sport about joining in. She said when one of the counselors used a table as a makeshift stage to play his guitar, it came to her that a real stage area would be a good addition to the camp. And a whole lot safer than a table."

Boy, what he wouldn't give to know what Priscilla's contribution to the talent show had been. "You said ideas. As in plural. What else did she come up with?"

"An organic garden and—"

"A what? A garden?"

Bobby nodded. "We used the area behind the dining hall. Already have the soil turned over and it'll be ready for the next group of campers to do the initial planting. Not sure how many vegetables we're going to get seeing as how we're starting this late in the summer, but the kids will have fun. That's what really counts."

Dean guessed he was right about that. So, a performance stage and a garden. He wondered what else she'd come up with. "Anything else?"

"You know that blank interior wall between the office and the camp store? The one where we talked about having a mural painted?"

Dean remembered. "Didn't Leeann mention getting someone local to do it? Please don't tell me Priscilla suggested something along the likes of a Picasso or a Renoir?"

"Very funny. No, she thought we should cover that area with chalkboard paint and allow the campers to provide the artwork instead. We can assign each cabin a set number of days when their work would be displayed, take photographs of whatever design they come up with to keep for the camp's photo albums and then wash it off so the space is ready for the next masterpiece."

Dean had to admit the idea was a good one. A great one.

What kid wouldn't like to walk by and see his artwork on display for the entire camp to enjoy?

"You should've seen her and Leeann yesterday when they painted the wall. By the time I got here, I think they had more paint on themselves than anywhere else." Bobby laughed. "Priscilla readily admitted she had no experience with a paintbrush outside of an art class here or there, but— Ah, there she is, and looking paint-free today."

They'd stopped beside the area for the outdoor stage, but Dean's gaze was already centered on the tall woman leading a horse from the nearby stable into the smaller of two attached corrals. He immediately picked up on the rider as being Holly Warren, a sweet kid and one of Dean's favorite campers. Her mother was the camp's nurse, meaning Holly was often here even during the off weeks. Due to a neuromuscular disease that left her right leg weak, she wore a brace full-time but she never let the impediment stop her from being fully involved with all camp activities.

The girl's infectious giggle could be heard clear over where he and Bobby stood, but it was Priscilla who captured Dean's attention.

Holding the reins of the pony with ease, she seemed to be speaking to both the four-legged creature and to Holly. Priscilla looked just like any other member of the staff, but was stunningly beautiful in an outfit far different than her usual style.

Jean shorts made her long legs look even longer, while a plaid shirt, sleeves rolled back to her elbows, hung loose and unbuttoned—he guessed she had a T-shirt on underneath. A straw cowboy hat of all things sat perched on her head with her blond waves pulled back into a low ponytail at the nape of her neck.

It seemed she'd also captured Daisy's attention, too.

The dog took off toward the corral, trotting straight for her friend.

"Daisy, halt." Dean's voice was low, but the command was firm. "Stay."

This time his pet actually listened, stopping just outside the wood fencing and planting her butt on the grass. Her tail wagged hard, but she stayed put. Both Holly and Priscilla looked their way when Dean called out, and offered a quick wave in their direction before turning back to their lesson.

"Hey, buddy." Bobby waved back but then snapped his fingers a couple of times in front of Dean's face. "You still with me?"

He was, but he couldn't take his eyes off Priscilla. Her ease with the animal was evident, but what he couldn't get over was how right the princess looked in that getup. He couldn't tell what she wore on her feet from this distance, but he'd bet it wasn't the sexy heels she'd claimed to be able to run a marathon in.

"Hey, I forget to tell you," Bobby continued. "A bunch of the guys are coming over to the house tonight for barbecue, beer and to watch the ball game. I know you've had a long week, but you're welcome to join us."

If Bobby was talking about the usual crowd, that would be at least five or six men. "You sure Lee is going to be up for all that company?"

"Oh, she's going out with the girls tonight to the Blue Creek." Bobby's grin widened. "They're taking Priscilla out for her birthday."

And the surprises just kept coming. "It's her birthday?"

"The actual date was a couple of days ago, I guess, but she let it slip this morning to Lee and soon a girls' night out was in the works. Lee gets to be the designated driver, of course."

As hard as he tried, Dean just couldn't picture Priscilla knocking back a few beers with Leeann and her friends at the local saloon, even though he'd offered to take her to dinner at to the Blue Creek—what, two weeks ago?

Wow, had it really been that short of a time since they'd met? How had she so easily found her way into his daily thoughts? Sure, he'd been attracted to her from the moment he'd seen her, but how much did he really know about her?

She took her job seriously despite obviously rolling in dough. She wasn't afraid to join in and get her hands dirty. She had a sense of humor that she tried to hide after her clumsiness during the tour had him saving her from spiders and taking a dunk in the lake.

He also knew a couple of people very close to her had hurt her deeply. She was obviously nursing a bruised heart.

"So, you interested in tonight?" Bobby asked.

"Yeah, sounds good. Count me in."

"I'm heading back to the office to check on my wife. You coming?"

Dean glanced at his friend, not surprised by the smug grin on his face. "Yeah, I think I will. I want to congratulate the new mama with a big hug."

The arrogance disappeared from Bobby's expression as he glanced over at the corral for a moment. "Okay, well, I should warn you. Priscilla's dog, Snake, is in the office with Leeann. He seems as infatuated with my wife as Daisy is with your—with Priscilla."

Yeah, and Dean was finally realizing Daisy wasn't the only infatuated one around here. The question was, what was he going to do about it?

The answer: nothing.

She was only in town for another few weeks and then

she and her dog would hop into her sporty little convertible and drive off into the sunset. Alone.

He'd walked away.

After hearing Dean call out to his dog, Priscilla had been sure he'd come down to the corral to at least say hello to her and Holly. Instead, he'd whistled for Daisy to join him, but the dog had given her owner a quick glance over one shoulder and stayed put just outside the corral as Dean headed for the dining hall with Bobby.

Not that his leaving had stopped Holly from chatting about "Mr. Zip" throughout the rest of the lesson.

"I think that young lady has a pretty big crush on your master." Priscilla sat on one of the benches that lined the back porch of the dining hall, Daisy at her side. She gave the dog a quick scratch behind the ear, noticing her fingers were long overdue for a manicure. "Not that it's hard to see why. Holly might only be nine years old, but she can list Dean's attributes better than any dating website. Smart, caring, good-looking, funny—"

Daisy gave out a quick bark.

"And he's got a great dog." Priscilla laughed when she nodded in agreement. "You know, Daisy, I think you're a bit misunderstood when it comes to your aversion to females. You were very nice on the walk back from the barn with Holly."

This time Daisy dipped her snout, but looked up at Priscilla with sorrowful eyes. "What happened, girl? Was someone not nice to you once upon a time?"

This time Daisy looked away and let out a sigh as she laid down, her paws hanging over the edge of the bench.

"Don't want to talk about it, huh? That's okay. Girl to girl, I understand." Priscilla stretched out herself, crossing her legs at the ankles. "Sometimes talk is overrated. Sometimes it's best to let actions speak louder than words. And boy, have we had an active day."

It'd been a long day—a long week—but a very fulfilling one. She'd worked harder physically this past week than she'd done in years. Daily yoga classes and a few miles on the treadmill had her thinking she'd been in great shape, but the things she'd been doing around Camp Diamond had really given her a workout. And it felt good.

Not just the idle muscles that were slowly getting used to being active again, but deeper, in her heart and in her mind, where it counted even more.

She'd felt more useful digging in the dirt, painting walls and working in the stables with the horses than she had in the past few months at her office at the foundation. Even the bachelor auction was coming together nicely, mostly because everyone involved—from the committee members to the bachelors—all believed in the end goal of helping the camp.

Not that the organizations she worked with back home didn't aspire to the same thing, but there always seemed to be at least two or three people who excelled at cageyness and gamesmanship that would often make pulling together an event more difficult than it needed to be. It'd been happening so frequently that Priscilla had felt only relief once the fund-raisers were over.

Not this time. She was enjoying her stay in Destiny, enjoying being here at the camp. Which was something she'd never expected that first day when she'd arrived—

"Boy, you must be a million miles away. Dreaming of a sun-soaked beach or shopping on Rodeo Drive?"

Startled, Priscilla looked up to find Dean leaning against one of the porch posts. Her breath caught in her chest. What had Holly called him? Oh, yes. A cutie-pie. Yes, he was that. "Oh! Hello. I didn't hear you come up."

"So where's your watchdog?"

She grinned. "Snake is with Leeann. He rarely leaves her side anymore. Especially after she announced her pregnancy— Oh! I hope I didn't ruin the surprise. Did you know?"

"Yes, Bobby told me earlier today." He pointed to the bench. "Mind if I join you?"

A thrill raced through her that seemed so silly she ignored it. "Please do. I'm just waiting for Leeann to finish up a phone call."

"I heard about your plans for tonight." Dean sat on the other side of Daisy, who propped her head on his thigh. "So you're finally going to visit the famous Blue Creek Saloon."

"I've already been there."

"Really?"

"Last weekend. Checking out the setup for the auction. Of course, it was the middle of the afternoon, so I'm guessing it won't be as quiet this evening." She smiled, remembering Leeann's plans for tonight. "It seems Leeann and her friends are determined to teach me to line dance. But I must say, you were right. The burgers there are wonderful."

Dean leaned back and propped his elbow on the back of the bench. "Well, look at you. Manual labor, hanging out in bars..." He tapped the curved brim of the straw cowboy hat she wore. "Even your clothes are looking a bit different these days. Has the city princess turned into a country girl?"

She'd forgotten about the hat, an impulse buy while shopping last week. Yanking it off, she pushed back her hair, which had fallen free of the ponytail and into her face. "It helps protect my skin from the sun, especially when I'm outside with the horses."

"You looked pretty comfortable down there."

Priscilla kept her gaze on the hat resting in her lap. "I've loved horses since I was a little girl. I'm more used to an English saddle—"

"Gee, now, there's a surprise."

She looked up. He was teasing her, but instead of getting defensive—her standard operating procedure—she returned his smile. "I know, right? But I do have some experience with Western and, well, a horse is a horse. You know, Holly was disappointed you didn't come down to say hi earlier."

"Yeah, she made that pretty clear when I saw her head out with her mom." Dean leaned in close and lowered his voice to whisper, "Personally, I think she was looking for someone else to help with her barn duties, like dishing out the horses' grain."

Priscilla laughed. "You're probably right about that. But we were able to handle it, which means I am in desperate need of a bath before I go out tonight."

"You've been working hard around here this week."

She nodded. "Yes, I'm exhausted, but it's a good kind of tired."

"I wanted to tell you that I think you've come up with some pretty good ideas for the camp. And it's not just me. Bobby and Leeann are impressed as well, since they put them all into action."

His approval made her go all soft inside. She'd only attended the weekly staff meeting as an observer, but once again found herself unable to stop from offering up her ideas. "Even the performance pavilion?"

Dean laughed. "Yes, even that. But I've got to ask you, what was the talent you performed at the show with the kids?"

A hot blush flooded her cheeks. "Oh, it was nothing. Just something silly. I wasn't even going to join in, but the kids dared me."

"You have to tell me now."

She rolled her eyes but saw the determination in his, so she said, "I peeled the skin off of an apple with a sharp knife in one continuous piece."

"One complete length? No breaks? That is pretty impressive."

"It's a skill I acquired one summer from our cook. I used to sit at the kitchen counter for hours and peel the apples she needed for her pies." Priscilla smiled as the long-ago memory came back to her. "My mother always said the only thing she ever made in the kitchen was menus for her dinner parties, but Adelina had insisted my sister and I know our way around the stove."

"I'm guessing this is the same sister who—"

Priscilla stood. Talking about Jacqueline, even thinking about her, was the last thing she wanted right now. "I should probably go find—"

"Hey, hold on a minute." Dean laid a hand on her arm, stopping her escape. "I'm sorry. I shouldn't have said anything."

"It's okay."

"No, it's not, but please don't go yet. I have something for you."

His tone was so sincere, she sat back down.

He patted Daisy on her rump and the dog jumped down from the bench and sat at his feet. He then stretched out his right leg and, reaching into the oversize side cargo pocket of his shorts, pulled out a cellophane-wrapped cupcake. He quickly unwrapped the packaging and held the treat out toward her in the palm of his hand. "Sorry if it's a little squished. I know it's not much, but it's the best I could do under such short notice."

She looked down at the chocolate cupcake with its familiar white loopy scroll across the top. "I don't understand."

"Bobby told me that it's— And, well, you're going out to celebrate—" He broke off and gave a halfhearted shrug. "Hell, everyone deserves cake on their birthday, even if it's a small one."

Stunned, Priscilla stared at the snack and blinked back sudden tears.

When she and Leeann had been talking earlier about the baby's due date, somehow the discussion had gotten around to zodiac signs, with Priscilla revealing she was a moon child and her birthday had been just two days ago. Leeann had then insisted that they go out tonight to celebrate, and she would get her friends—a few of them whom Priscilla had already met—to join them. Other than a beautiful bouquet of flowers from Lisa that had arrived for her at the inn on Wednesday and an electronic greeting card from her assistant, no one else—meaning neither her father nor Jacqueline—had acknowledged her special day.

"Oh, Dean. You didn't have to do this."

"It's no big deal. Just don't expect me to sing, okay?"

She laughed and looked up at him. "Hmm, it's just not a birthday cake without the song."

Dean reached into another pocket of his cargo shorts and, with the flick of his thumbnail, ignited the wooden matchstick he held in his hand. He then stuck it into the top of the cupcake. "How about a candle? Will that do?"

Priscilla didn't know what to say.

"Well, come on, before it burns out."

"What do you mean?"

Dean moved the cupcake closer. "What's a birthday cake without a wish?"

"I haven't made a wish on my birthday in years. I wouldn't— I don't have any idea what to wish for."

"Anything your heart desires. That's what makes wishes

so cool." A grin tugged at his mouth. "And since it's been so long, you better make it count."

Priscilla returned Dean's stare for a moment, then closed her eyes. She never did get to make that request in the church that first Sunday, but this time she wished on the first thought that came to her. She then opened her eyes, puckered her lips and blew out the makeshift candle.

Dean smiled and gently placed the snack cake in her hand. "I hope your wish was a good one."

Oh, it was, but would it ever come true? Probably not, but hey, a girl could hope, and wasn't that what wishes were for?

Chapter Eight

"You know, the last time I drank out of a shot glass was probably in college, but these birthday-cake thingies are so good." Priscilla reached for another one of the festive drinks in the center of the table. "What's in this again?"

"Frangelico and vanilla-flavored vodka. Here, don't forget the lemon." Racy Steele, the owner of the Blue Creek Saloon and wife to the town's sheriff, held out the sugar-frosted piece of fruit. "It's nothing without this."

Priscilla took the lemon slice and, along with the other ladies at the table, except for Leeann, who was drinking only ice water tonight, raised her glass in salute before downing another shot.

The first time they'd done this, Priscilla had been the last one to set her glass on the table and bite into the lemon. This time she was the first and it had only taken her—she counted the empty upside-down glasses in front of her—four tries to accomplish that feat. Considering she still wasn't getting the hang of dancing in a straight line to country music, Priscilla enjoyed this victory.

"Boy, you're getting a little too good at this," Maggie Cartwright said, laughing. She was Leeann's other best friend—besides Racy—and ran a ranch outside of town she shared with her husband, daughter and toddler son. "Maybe we should slow down."

"No kidding," Racy's sister-in-law, Gina Dillon, added. "I bet the guys aren't going through as much alcohol tonight as we are."

"They might be. It's been a while since either Gage or I have had an evening away from the twins. And they turned two this past spring." Racy waved over one of her waitresses, who cleared the table of the empties, replacing them with another round of beers.

"Same goes for me," said Maggie. "Between chasing after horses and trying to keep up with Tyler, who's just a few months older than Racy's kids, Landon and I haven't had too many nights out, either."

"So all of you are relatively new moms?" Priscilla looked around the table. "With Leeann of course being the newest mommy."

"I guess so." Gina grabbed her beer. "I've been a stepmom since Justin and I married last year, but we've only got one more court appearance before my petition to adopt Jacoby is finalized. Of course, he's already bugging us for a little brother or sister."

"Oh, that's wonderful news about the adoption!" Racy leaned over and gave Gina a big hug. "You have been so wonderful with Jacoby from the very beginning. I know you'll be just as terrific with a new baby. Besides, my brother isn't getting any younger. And neither are you."

"Hey! I'm not even close to thirty yet," Gina protested,

but her smile was full of mischief. "Unlike the rest of you. I'm still the baby at this table."

Priscilla joined in the laughter and took another swallow of the icy-cold beer. Straight from the bottle. Another first for her in a long time. She had to admit she'd been a bit nervous about tonight's plans, but Leeann's friends were all great women and she was having a blast. So many people had come up to their table throughout the evening to talk about the auction and the camp. She'd even run into two of Dean's fellow firefighters she'd met at bingo, but turned down both of their requests for a dance.

"You know, just because the rest of us aren't interested in slow dancing doesn't mean you have to sit out when asked," Racy said.

"Yeah, you're a pretty popular lady. Must be because you're the mysterious out-of-towner." Maggie took a swallow of her beer and looked around the bar. "Nothing like new blood in town to bring out the cowboys."

"Or the cops or the firemen." Leeann leaned forward, wrapping her hands around her glass. "Especially one fireman in particular."

"Are we talking about Zip?" Gina chimed in. "Now, there's one hunky guy."

"Do we have a new romance in the works?" Maggie asked.

Priscilla shook her head and then suddenly wished she hadn't when the room took an interesting tilt. "No. Dean and I are just…"

"Friends?" All four ladies asked in unison.

"We're…well, we're working together on the auction. Working together at the camp. Sort of. So I guess we're…" Priscilla snapped her mouth closed when she realized a few too many seconds had gone by without her finishing that sentence. By the amused looks on the ladies' faces, it didn't really matter what she was about to say. But she said it anyway. "Yes, we're friends."

"Does that mean there's no chance of you bidding on him at the auction?" Racy asked.

"He hasn't said what his date package will be yet," Leeann said, then smiled. "Maybe she's waiting to find out how creative he gets before she makes up her mind."

"Married or not, I think my hubby is going to have to step it up when it comes to planning a date night for the two of us." Gina raised her beer in the air. "Anybody else with me?"

The ladies all clicked their bottles in agreement, Priscilla included, and the talk turned to the various dates planned by the bachelors participating in the auction. Listening to the women debate the various offerings reminded Priscilla of that simple yet special moment back at the camp with Dean this afternoon.

"Priscilla? You ready for another lesson?"

Leeann, Racy, Maggie and Gina all stood up from the table. She groaned. "Another lesson in scoot booting?"

Leeann laughed. "It's called boot scooting, and yes, it is. Grab that cowboy hat and let's get back out on the dance floor."

"Are you sure this is a good idea?" Dean looked over at Bobby, who sat in the passenger side of his truck.

The cupcake had been stupid. Schmaltzy and stupid, even though Priscilla had seemed to enjoy his gesture. But this latest idea was probably taking things a bit too far.

"Are you asking me if I think Leeann is going to tell me I'm being a bit overprotective? Yeah, probably." Bobby leaned forward and peered out into the crowded parking lot. "But it was Maggie who texted Landon and said their evening was coming to an end and that she and Gina were heading out."

"She also said Priscilla was acting a bit loopy. Whatever the hell that means."

"I think it means she had a good time." Bobby pointed at a group of women heading out into the parking lot from the bar's double doors. "Which I don't have a problem with—"

"But you'd rather Leeann not be the one who has to get Priscilla back to her room at the inn."

Bobby pushed open his door and grinned. "Precisely. Thanks for agreeing to make sure she gets home okay. Even though I had to twist your arm."

Dean kept his mouth shut as he got out from behind the wheel. There had been no arm-twisting. Hell, it'd been his idea to come here and make sure the girls got home okay even though they knew Leeann hadn't been drinking tonight.

He and Bobby headed across the parking lot toward Leeann and Priscilla, who were walking their way, giggling over a private joke.

"Have fun tonight, ladies?" Bobby called out.

"Bobby!" Leeann halted and slapped a hand to her chest. "You scared me. What are you two doing here?"

"Our evening ended and you all were still out having fun. We figured we'd come down and join you."

Dean glanced at his friend. *Good line, buddy.*

"Well, our party has just ended, too." Priscilla flung her arms out wide. "You boys are too late to join in the fun."

"I don't know about that," Dean said under his breath.

"It's not polite to whisper, you know." Priscilla propped her hands on her hips, causing her to take a couple of steps backward in order to keep her balance. "What did you say?"

Dean walked a few steps closer until he stood right in

front of her. "I said I think it's time for Cinderella to get home before the clock strikes midnight."

"It's still an hour until then." Priscilla pointed to her fancy gold watch.

"But I got tired," Leeann added, "so the party broke up early."

"How about I take you home and tuck you into bed?" Bobby put an arm around his wife's shoulders and pulled her close to his side. "Dean will make sure Priscilla gets back to the inn in one piece."

"Are you okay with that, Priscilla?" Leeann asked.

"Sure. Whatever. You go on home with your hubby."

Leeann turned to Dean. "She's had a few drinks."

"Just a few?" Dean smiled. "Don't worry. I'll make sure the princess gets back to her castle."

Priscilla and Leeann hugged goodbye, whispering among themselves and sharing another laugh. Then Leeann and Bobby headed toward Leeann's car, and Dean turned to Priscilla and pointed at his truck.

"Your pumpkin awaits."

The hands were back on her hips again as she stared at him for a long moment. She swayed a bit, but stayed upright. Dean wondered when the last time she'd been like this was. It had probably been years. Before he could ask, she marched across the parking lot, giving him a very nice view of her backside thanks to those shorts of hers.

Bellissima! He followed and waited as she waved off his hand and climbed up into the passenger seat. By the time he got around to the driver's side, she'd dropped her hat in the space between them and buckled her seat belt. He pulled out of the parking lot and headed down Main Street.

"Do you mind the windows being down?" Dean asked.

Priscilla sat with her head back against the headrest, eyes closed. "No, the cool air feels good."

He drove well under the speed limit, as it would only take a few minutes to get back to the inn and he found himself, once again, wanting to spend time with her. "Hey, have you been to Sherry's Diner? They serve a great cup of coffee—"

"Oh, I almost forgot." Priscilla sat up straight and opened her eyes. "We need to go back to the camp."

That came out of nowhere. "What for?"

"I forgot Snake's pillow there this afternoon. He's going to have a hard time sleeping tonight without it."

"Are you serious? A pillow?"

She nodded vigorously, then put a hand to her head. "Leeann and I had planned to stop by when we left the bar. Do you mind?"

No, he didn't mind at all. Anything to be able to spend a few more minutes with her. "Sure, let's get the pillow."

Dean took the turn off the town square and headed toward the camp. The roads out there were dark, and with the only light coming from his truck's dashboard, he couldn't tell if Priscilla was asleep or not as she'd once again leaned back against the seat.

Eventually he turned into the camp, glad they had installed the security lighting on each of the buildings. He pulled to a stop outside the dining hall and shut down his truck. The camp was practically deserted. The only staff here during the off week were a few college-aged counselors from out of town and Sylvie, the camp director, who had her own cabin nestled away in the trees near the sports area.

"Priscilla, we're here." No response. "You awake?"

"Awake. Sure, I'm awake."

The slight slur of her words and the fact she hadn't moved an inch told Dean she really wasn't. He sighed and released his seat belt. "I'll go look for the pillow. Are you going to be okay out here?"

Priscilla gave a little wiggle, as if she were snuggling deeper into the seat. "Hmm. Yes, I'm okay."

Figuring it was easier—not to mention probably quicker—to do this himself, Dean got out of the truck. He headed up the front steps of the main camp building, stopping to look back and check on Priscilla. He then unlocked the doors and slipped inside. Entering the office, he flipped on the overhead light and hunted around. He had no idea what the mutt's pillow looked like, but since Daisy herself had a cushion bed, he assumed it must be similar. It took him more than half a dozen passes around the office before he found the stuffed pillow monogrammed with a capital *S*.

Shaking his head, he grabbed the thing and closed up the office. He went back outside, locked the door and started for his truck. His empty truck. He raced across the yard, praying she was stretched out on the seat. When he got to the passenger side, all he found inside the cab was her cowboy hat.

Where in the hell had she disappeared to?

The woman was just drunk enough to be a danger to herself. Fear seized his chest, but he fought it off. He hadn't been gone that long. She couldn't have gotten far. "Priscilla?" he called out, not having to raise his voice much for the sound to be carried across the quiet night. "Priscilla, where are you?"

"I'm down he-re." Her singsong voice floated back to him. "Isn't it a beaut-beautiful night?"

Dean followed the sound of her voice. Thanks to the brightness of the full moon, he immediately spotted her about fifty yards away, walking across the open field and heading straight for the beach area by the lake. He tossed the pillow inside his truck and took off after her. By the time he reached her, she was already out of her boots and ankle-deep into the lake.

"Going for a swim?"

He should be pissed at her. Hell, he was already mad at himself for leaving her alone, but she looked so familiar, yet different, standing there, lazily walking back and forth in the water, much like the first time he'd seen her. She was still very much a water nymph, as tempting and alluring as that day down by the river, but now she seemed…

Relaxed. Comfortable. Approachable.

While he was sure whatever she'd consumed tonight contributed to that, she had been the same way earlier today sitting on the bench outside the dining hall with him and Daisy.

"Do you believe in wishes?"

Priscilla's soft-spoken question pulled him from his thoughts. "I don't know. Do you?"

"I mean when you were a kid. You must've wished on birthday candles, sent letters to Santa Claus, searched for a shooting star on nights like this."

Dean stood at the water's edge and crossed his arms over his chest. He thought back to his childhood and how certain toys always made it under the tree or appeared at birthday parties. How he and his brothers and sisters had many magical moments in their youth, from family camping trips to dinners around the large kitchen table. "Yeah, I guess I've had a few come true in my lifetime."

Priscilla's sigh was dramatic as she continued to pace back and forth, splashing in the water. "You're lucky. I've never had one come true."

"Never?"

She shook her head. "Once when I was six years old I wished for a pony. I had just started taking riding lessons that summer and I really wanted one of my own. A white one. Just like the one the prince rides in the fairy tales. I made sure both my parents and my nanny knew, but that wish never came true. Unless you count the Thoroughbred racehorse my father bought for me that Christmas."

He wasn't sure how to respond to that, so he just said, "Well, I guess you could consider that a wish sort of coming true."

"Not to me. But I really gave up believing in wishes when I was sixteen." She looked over at him. "Do you want to know why?"

Dean had a feeling she wasn't talking about what most kids that age wanted—four wheels and a driver's license. "Sure."

"My mom got sick the year before. Well, she'd been ill for a while but they told us right after my fifteenth birthday. And though I guess, deep inside, I knew it wouldn't help, I wished on a star every night, wished on my birthday, even wrote a letter to God and tucked it under my pillow for the next six months...but she died just before Halloween the following year. Then it was just my father, my sister and me. And a house full of servants, of course."

As someone who considered himself blessed to have parents who were still around, not to mention happily married, a handful of brothers and sisters and an eighty-three-year-old grandmother who was vibrant and full of life, Dean had no idea what to say. "I'm sorry, Priscilla. It must've been tough to lose her when you were so young."

She stopped and looked over at him. "Thank you for saying that." She started walking again but this time she came toward him. "You know, it was you who got me thinking about wishes again. Well, you and Minnie Gates."

Dean wasn't sure what the proprietor of the Painted Lady had to do with this conversation, but he didn't like that what he'd done this afternoon had brought back such bad memories for Priscilla. "Again, I'm sorry. I didn't mean to make you feel bad by asking you to make a wish on that silly match."

"You didn't. Please, don't think that way." Priscilla laid a hand on his arm. "What you did for me was one of the nicest surprises I've had in a long time and I enjoyed making that wish."

She suddenly seemed far too sober and he found himself wanting more than anything to believe her.

"What if I told you that *you* have the power to make my wish come true?"

At this moment he'd move heaven and earth to give her whatever she asked. "Name it."

Her eyes widened in surprise. "Really?"

He nodded. "Whatever you want. It's yours."

"Okay, then." She peered up at him for a long moment and then took a deep breath. "What I want is for you to kiss me."

Dean wasn't sure he'd heard her correctly. Her voice was soft and she was, if not slurring her words, blending them together from time to time. "Excuse me?"

She dropped her hand. "Are you going to make me say it again?"

Damn straight. "I want to be sure."

Her lips curved up in an enticing smile. "My wish was for a birthday kiss. From you."

"Are you sure you want one from me?" Jeez, he couldn't believe he'd just asked that. "What I mean is—"

"That's okay." She backed away, deeper into the water. "I knew it was silly. Don't worry about it. I wouldn't want you to do anything you don't want—"

Ignoring the familiar feeling of water in his shoes, Dean reached Priscilla in three steps and pulled her into his arms, aware once again of how perfectly her curves fit along every inch of his body. He crooked his elbow around her waist and tunneled the fingers of his other hand into her hair, tilting her head upward until their eyes met. The moonlight allowed him to see her surprise but also the desire in her gaze. He wanted to prolong this moment, to let the anticipation build, but when she moistened her lips with the sweep of her tongue, he was lost.

Slanting his mouth over hers, he forced himself to keep the kiss light and simple when deep inside there was nothing simple about this woman. Her low groan reached his ears at the same moment as her fingers grabbed at his shirt, her hands curling into tight fists. Still, he resisted the urge to pull her hard against his chest and deepen the kiss. Then the tip of her tongue danced along the seam of his lips. Powerless to ignore her request, he allowed her entrance and met her halfway with a silken stroke of his own. He loved how she tasted like a hint of vanilla. Fire and passion flared between them as she returned his kiss, spurring the almost uncontrollable need that spread through his blood.

He finally pulled back to gulp down a couple of breaths. Not wanting to let her go, he tucked her head beneath his chin as she wrapped her arms around his back. They stood like that for a long moment while he struggled to regain his composure.

"Happy Birthday, Priscilla," he finally said, his words a rough whisper.

Her only response was her steady breathing, and the slackening of her embrace forced him to tighten his own grip to keep her upright. He gave a rueful shake of his head when he realized what had happened.

His princess had fallen asleep.

As hard as she tried to ignore the bright light pressing against her eyelids, it was the heavenly scent of freshly brewed coffee that forced Priscilla to accept the need to wake up. That and the fact that it felt as if she was sleeping on a rock.

She rolled over, the scratchy feel of the blanket against her skin unfamiliar. Placing her hand over her eyes, she managed to open one just a slit and, through spread fingers, took in the large desk surrounded by log walls directly in front of her.

Where was she? And why did her head feel as if a thousand horses were galloping across her brain?

"Good morning, sunshine." A pair of jean-clad legs stepped into her line of vision. "Time to rise and greet a beautiful new day."

Familiar legs. Familiar voice. Familiar office.

Priscilla groaned and closed her eyes again despite the heavenly aroma that was even closer now. "Please tell me that coffee's heavily laced with low-fat cream and three sugars."

"Sorry. I should've known you'd like it sweet, but this is strictly black."

"I don't care." It felt as if her head weighed twice her total body weight, but she managed to push herself into a sitting position. "Hand it over."

"Please?"

She forced her eyes open again in time to watch the wool blanket slip from her lap, revealing that she was wearing the same outfit she'd put on to go out with the girls—

Oh, boy. So that's what happened last night.

Looking up, she found Dean leaning against his desk, holding two mugs of steaming coffee in his hands, a smile on his too-handsome face. His hair was damp, as if he'd just finished taking a shower, but how could that be? And what had he asked from her again? All she could focus on at the moment was her body's need for caffeine. "I am so hoping one of those is for me...please."

He handed her a mug.

She inhaled the enticing fragrance, already feeling the java work its magic. "I can't believe how much I had to drink last night. I haven't done that in years."

"From what I could tell—"

She winced and held up a hand in a silent plea.

"From what I've heard, you enjoyed yourself," Dean continued in a softer tone laced with humor. "Something about birthday-cake shots?"

Yes, last night's activities were coming back to her, but that didn't explain how she ended up sleeping on a couch in Dean's office at the camp's health center. She remembered being better at drinking than line dancing and then giving Leeann a hug goodbye in the bar's parking lot. Dean had been there, too, just like he was here now, but why had he brought her out to the camp instead of taking her back to the inn?

"I don't understand. How did we end up here?"

Dean's hand stilled as he was about to take a sip. He lowered the mug away from his mouth. "You don't remember what we did?"

Her mouth went dry. *What they did?* "I remember being with the girls, meeting up with you and Bobby in the parking lot." Priscilla fought hard for the memories. "Riding in your truck…"

"That's it?" The humor in his eyes and the smile on his face vanished as her voice faded. "You don't recall anything that happened after that?"

A blinding panic filled her. Had she done something stupid? Pulled a Jacqueline-size scandal? Something that this time was entirely her fault? "Please tell me I didn't do anything wrong or embarrassing or—"

"Relax, you didn't." Dean took a sip from his mug and

continued, "Even if you had, nobody in Destiny would care one way or the other."

Maybe not in Destiny, but there were plenty of people who'd love to catch her in a bumbling or awkward moment that would be featured on entertainment news shows or websites. Relief flowed through her veins as she placed the mug to her lips and took a small sip of the potent liquid. "Thank goodness, but that still doesn't explain what I'm doing in your office."

"You really don't remember the two of us down by the lake? Talking? Your birthday wish?"

"My birthday..." She pressed her fingertips to the spot between her eyes where it felt as if the Los Angeles Philharmonic Orchestra was playing Mozart's *Rondo Alla Turca* at twice the normal speed. "I made a birthday wish?"

As soon as the words moved past her lips, it came back to her how she had indeed done exactly that yesterday afternoon when Dean had so sweetly offered her the opportunity thanks to a store-bought cupcake and a wooden match.

"Yes, of course, I remember making a wish—but I didn't tell you— Oh!" The mug tilted and the coffee splashed precariously against the rim. She sat it on the small table in front of her with a thud and covered her eyes with her hands. "Oh, no! I did tell you! I did more than tell you. I asked you to make my wish come true."

"Oh, you did." Wry amusement laced his voice. "It's nice to know it was so memorable."

It had been that and more. Piece by piece the memories of her actions last night came flooding back. The two of them by the water, sharing stories about childhood wishes, and then her suddenly being brave enough to tell him what she'd really wished for on that cupcake.

Her heart pounded in her chest as she relived the panic when she thought he was turning her down. The passion that had engulfed her when he'd pulled her into his arms and put his mouth over hers. The kiss had started out soft and sweet, tentative, even, but when she'd sensed he was pulling away, she'd been the one to take things to the next level. With a quick swipe of her tongue, she'd asked for more and he'd readily complied, and that simple kiss had become something sensual and exciting and overpowering until the overwhelming need for air—

How could she have forgotten a single second of that amazing moment?

"I can't believe I did that," she muttered. "Alcohol and losing one's inhibitions are never a good mix."

"Boy, you sure know how to stroke a guy's ego."

Dropping her hands, she clutched at her bare knees and forced herself to look him in the eye, despite the pounding in her head and the embarrassment burning through her veins. "This isn't about your ego. This is about self-respect. And I always, *always* carry myself with grace and dignity. Because of a few shots of alcohol, I forgot everything I swore to myself and could have made a huge mistake."

Like Jacqueline repeatedly did.

Hadn't she cleaned up enough of her sister's messes to know she had to always be focused? Yes, she was in Destiny. No paparazzi lurking in nearby bushes...but still. One trip in the headlines was enough for her, and the last thing she wanted was Dean's picture plastered all over the place, under bold print that read "Drunken Rejected Sister's Rebound."

She covered her face again and moaned.

"Don't worry about it, princess." He took another long swallow from his mug. "No harm, no foul, no big deal."

No big deal.

The casualness of his tone was like a sharp slice to her

gut. Priscilla staggered to her feet, the need to escape the laughter in his eyes wreaking havoc on her stomach.

Because to her—someone who'd been on the receiving end of damaging, impulsive behavior—it was a very big deal.

Chapter Nine

"Gentlemen, if I could have your attention, please. We plan to start in just a few minutes."

Priscilla spoke into the microphone attached to the podium on the left side of the stage at the Blue Creek Saloon. She looked over the crowded dance floor. There were a few ladies here and there, but the majority of the people in the bar on this Sunday afternoon were the bachelors for the auction that was only five days away. This was the second of two planned rehearsals. Leeann had thought the run-throughs might help the men feel more comfortable if they knew what was expected from them when the big night arrived.

But not all the bachelors had shown up. Dean was nowhere to be found.

He'd missed the first rehearsal for a perfectly valid reason. Bobby had explained that his absence then and around the camp all last week was due to a patient of his who was going through a difficult period, resulting in Dean being called away to the veterans' center in Cheyenne.

Was that why he wasn't here this afternoon? Or could it be something else?

She'd seen him this morning at church—granted, it had been from across the sanctuary, as he'd chosen not to sit with her, Bobby and Leeann. Yes, it'd been crowded in the row where they sat, but they could've made room for him. She'd tried not to take it personally, but ever since that morning when she'd made it clear how dismayed she'd been after remembering the kiss they'd shared—the kiss she'd asked for—they seemed to be back to square one when it came to being…friends?

More than friends?

She had no idea. All she knew was that she had embarrassed herself even further that morning by bolting for the bathroom. If she could've stayed hidden in there for hours she probably would have, but she'd left Snake alone all night at the inn and had needed to get back to him.

"I think we should get started now," Leeann said, pulling Priscilla from her thoughts as she joined her on the stage. "Most of the men who couldn't make it last time are here today and we have some that are back a second time. Perhaps Dean got caught up in saying goodbye to our latest group of campers."

"I thought maybe he might have gone to Cheyenne again."

Leeann frowned. "I suppose, but Bobby said something when we left church this morning about the two of them working on a project at the camp this afternoon. I've texted them, but neither has replied."

Priscilla nodded. This past week had been so much fun as Camp Diamond once again hosted local children. She'd helped out in the stables most days, with Holly by her side more often than not. The young girl had talked about Dean constantly, which matched Priscilla's relentless thoughts about the man as she tried to come to terms with her schoolgirl reaction to his kiss.

But Holly had really surprised her one day when she'd asked if there was an age limit on who could bid at the auction. At first, Priscilla thought perhaps she was going to bid on someone for her mother. Holly had giggled and said no, her mama was happily married even though Holly's dad was currently serving overseas with the army. As it turned out, Holly was looking to empty her piggy bank and place a bid on Dean for herself.

"Priscilla, did you hear me?" Leeann asked.

Shaking off the memory, Priscilla nodded. "Yes, of course."

She gripped her leather portfolio, turned the microphone over to Leeann and walked down the stairs to the dance floor, finding her steps a bit wobbly, as she was once again wearing high heels, having come here directly from church. Only this time her outfit was a simple cotton sundress with a matching lightweight cardigan sweater she'd picked up at a local shop. Today was the first time she'd worn a dress and heels in the past week, and while she wasn't uncomfortable, the desire to slip into a pair of jeans and a T-shirt was strong.

No matter her outfit, Priscilla felt more like herself as long as she concentrated on her job: the upcoming auction. "We covered some of what I'm about to say at the last rehearsal, but as everyone wasn't able to attend, please indulge me as I go over the basics again," she said, addressing the men directly. "We'll be handing out a list of the available bachelors with short bios and descriptions of your date packages to everyone who signs up to bid, and Leeann, our hostess and auctioneer for the evening, will be reading this information aloud when it's your turn."

She gestured toward the stage, using the moment to let her gaze sweep over the room as she still looked for Dean.

Leeann waved at everyone. "Don't worry. I'll make you all sound good."

Good-natured laughter rippled through the crowd. Priscilla waited for it to fade before she continued, "We are taking the traditional route with the auction, so bidders will be shouting out their dollar amounts, and of course, you all are welcome to encourage the ladies. But please be aware the event will be open to people of all ages." She thought back to Holly's plan. "We need to keep that in mind in case things get a little—"

"Rowdy?" one of the men offered with a grin.

"Yes, a perfect word. Rowdy," Priscilla said, smiling as the crowd's applause showed they agreed. "There will be time after the auction for socializing and to allow the bachelors and their winners to meet and perhaps set up a time and date to get together. As for who goes when, the committee is still deciding the order, mainly to mix up your professions so we don't have all the cowboys grouped together."

"Except for me," Willie Perkins, a cowboy who'd worked at Maggie Cartwright's ranch for the past fifty-plus years, called out from the center of the room. "This ol' cowboy is the first offering."

"Age before beauty," Liam Murphy joked, causing everyone to laugh.

"You're darn tootin'. I want to hook me a date before all you young bucks get out there and take all their money, leaving nothing for me."

Willie had celebrated his seventy-fifth birthday a few months ago, and according to Maggie, he still put in a full workday at her ranch. Priscilla had already been informed by the committee that there were quite a few members of the senior-citizen crowd who planned to bid on the gangly cowboy with his weathered skin and big smile.

"Yes, of course, Willie, you'll be first. Now, there will be a runway set up Friday night that will lead directly off the stage and out into the crowd," Priscilla continued, pointing toward the large rectangular outline taped in the middle of the dance floor. "Each bachelor will walk down three steps from the stage to the runway, continue on to the end, pause for a moment and then return back to where he started. If there's time, you're welcome to make a repeat journey."

"Let the ladies get a good look at the goods, right?"

"Or give them a chance to change their minds!"

"Hey, do you mind if we have a side bet on which one of us brings in the most money?"

Priscilla was glad to see the men were enjoying being part of the event. Some had seemed a bit shy about participating, but everyone knew all the money raised would be going to the camp, and the town had really stepped up to make this a great evening.

"Why don't we have the bachelors line up off to my right and we'll do a quick walk-through? After your turn, you're free to go. We'll see you back here Friday evening."

"I bet you can still make it to the rehearsal in time."

Dean ignored his friend while pretending to double check the safety harness he wore. He and Bobby had been working on the camp's challenge course, inspecting every rope, wire and fitting. They were twenty feet in the air, working on the last platform while Daisy supervised safely from the ground below.

"Or you could just continue giving me the silent treatment for the rest of the afternoon." Bobby leaned over and thumped Dean's helmet and then pointed to where Daisy marched back and forth, letting out a mournful howl every now and then. "Look, even your dog is worried. What's bothering you? Is it Branson?"

Even though he was officially on vacation for two weeks, Dean had made sure his patient and the staff at the veterans' center knew they could contact him anytime day or night if needed. There had been a few calls and Dean had either spoken to or gone back down to see Branson, seeing as how the young man had opened up to Dean more than anyone else when it came to his recent troubles.

"No, he seems to have turned a corner," Dean said, relieved that the kid had finally decided the best way to get over his wife leaving him was to be happy and healthy. "And Daisy is just worried that if something happens to me she won't know where her next meal is coming from."

"I'm glad to hear about your patient, but that's bull-hockey about your dog. Daisy knows I'll take care of her if something ever happens to you. She's even been warming up a bit toward Leeann."

Dean turned, sure he hadn't heard his buddy correctly. "Bull-hockey?"

Bobby shrugged. "I'm cutting down on the cussing. I promised the wife."

Grabbing the nearest wrench, Dean went back to work. Yeah, his friend did have a point. It seemed the more Daisy spent time at the camp with a certain beautiful blonde, the more tolerant she was becoming of females overall.

"Besides, we're thinking of getting a dog of our own," Bobby continued. Something small and manageable, like Snake. He seems to have appointed himself Leeann's guard-dog and the admiration is mutual."

"A dog and a baby? You're a braver man than me."

"That's not hard to believe. You won't go anywhere near Priscilla's pup."

That wasn't true. Dean had tried numerous times to make friends with the tiny mutt, but the one person at the camp that Snack—*Snake*—refused to associate with was him. Treats, toys, table scraps. It didn't matter. For whatever reason, the dog just didn't like him. Then again, the dog wasn't going to be around for much longer anyway.

"You know, I still don't get why you aren't down at the Blue Creek with the rest of the bachelors."

Dean sighed. He'd hoped his buddy had dropped the subject. "I said I would help with the course after the kids left today."

"And when I got Lee's first text message reminding me about the rehearsal, I told you we could finish this up another time."

"We were high off the ground and halfway through the course by then."

"Yeah, wasn't that convenient?"

Concentrating on tightening the last bolt, Dean remained silent.

"So, back to the auction. Have you come up with any exciting plans for your lucky winner yet?"

Dean didn't want to say anything until he worked out the final details. Besides, the auction was the last thing he wanted to talk about because it reminded him of Priscilla. Hell, everything reminded him of Priscilla. Despite his work with Branson in Cheyenne, he'd thought about her every day even though they hadn't had a moment alone together since that knock-his-boots-off, damned-if-he-didn't-want-to-do-it-all-over-again kiss.

A kiss she clearly wished hadn't happened at all.

"If you need any help getting creative, all you have to do is ask."

He gave the bolt one last hard twist, then turned to look at his friend. "I don't need any help."

Bobby returned his stare for a long moment, then packed up the rest of the tools and headed for the ladder. "You need something, man, but hell if I know what it is."

What Dean needed was his head examined for even thinking that night—that kiss—had meant something. It had to him. He remembered every single moment, from the second he'd seen her in the parking lot of the Blue Creek Saloon to when she'd fallen asleep right there in his arms.

Easily lifting her, he'd carried her back to his office at the health center. He'd tried several times to get her to wake up, but each time she'd moaned and groaned and gone right back to sleep. Then she'd finally awakened around sunrise and the last thing he'd expected was for her to react as if they'd done something wrong.

Dean shook off his thoughts and followed his buddy down the ladder until the two of them were on the ground and heading back to the maintenance shed, Daisy panting happily as she trotted alongside them. While they put the equipment away, Dean checked his watch. It was after four o'clock. The rehearsal had to be over by now. He probably should have gone, having already missed the first one, but then again, how difficult was it to walk around on a stage for a few minutes while a bunch of females decided how much they were willing to pay for a date with him?

"You ready to tell me what happened between you and Priscilla?"

His buddy's question had Dean catching his thumb in the door as he locked up the shed. "Ouch! Dammit!" Daisy barked as he pulled his hand free. Dean sent his dog a sharp look that quieted her while he shook away the pain. "What are you talking about?"

"It was a shot in the dark, but I seem to have hit the bull's-eye," Bobby said, then grinned. "As worried as you've been about Branson, somehow I figured our pretty blonde fund-raiser has more to do with your crappy attitude the last few days. Not to mention why you aren't down at the Blue Creek right now. What happened? Don't tell me you finally acted on the sparks flying between you two and she turned you down?"

Dean headed for the dining hall. "She didn't turn me down."

"Hey, score one for Romeo. Without going into any gory details, what happened?" Bobby asked, walking next to him. "Did you two make out like a couple teenagers in your truck that night after you took her home?"

"It wasn't in— Look, this is no big deal. It was just a kiss."

"Must've been some kiss. And what? You wanted more, but she didn't?"

Yeah, Dean could easily picture pulling Priscilla into his arms and kissing her again, that and a whole lot *more,* but she'd made it perfectly clear that just because someone wanted something didn't mean they always got it.

"More isn't the issue." Dean shook off the memory and followed Bobby into the office. They each grabbed a cold drink from the refrigerator and Dean then flopped down in the closest chair. Daisy jumped into his lap and he gave her a quick scratch before opening the soda and taking a long swallow.

Bobby mirrored his movements, but with an expectant look on his face as he waited.

"She didn't remember." Dean finally said the words aloud, keeping his gaze firmly planted on the condensation drops forming on the bottle in his hand. "Kissing me, I mean. Me kissing her. At first, anyway."

"Meaning what? You had to remind her?" Bobby asked.

Dean nodded, then dropped his head back against the

back of the chair and closed his eyes. "Yeah, let's just say her response wasn't what I expected."

"A blow to the male pride, huh?"

Bobby could say that again.

"What are you going to do about it?" his friend asked.

Dean didn't have any idea. "Any suggestions?"

"You're thinking too much. What's that saying? If at first you don't succeed, try, try again?"

"Are you saying I should ask for the second chance to make a better impression?"

Bobby shrugged. "Either that or just grab the woman and kiss her. What's the worst that could happen?"

She'd haul off and smack him? Or worse, tell him she regretted making her birthday wish in the first place? Either way, Dean decided he had to have an answer to those questions. Now.

Priscilla sat on a stool at the end of the bar, looking over her notes. She turned around every now and then to watch the bachelors on parade, not sure who was having more fun, the men or Leeann as she praised their virtues and the creative date packages each offered.

A buzzing noise caught Priscilla's ear and she dug for her cell phone. The display read Lennox Corporation. She sighed, assuming it was her father's secretary doing her weekly check-in call. Sliding off the stool, she quickly walked to the small alcove outside the restrooms. She hit the button and put the phone to her ear. "Hello, Elizabeth. How can I help you?"

"Priscilla, it's your father."

Shock at hearing the deep, resonating tone of Harold Lennox for the first time in almost a month had Priscilla bracing herself against a nearby table.

"Priscilla? Are you still there?"

"Yes, I'm still here, just surprised to hear your voice." She closed her eyes for a moment and pulled in a deep breath. "To what do I owe the pleasure?"

"Don't be impertinent with me, young lady. Not when I'm calling you from Paris in the middle of the night."

Priscilla quickly did the time change in her head. It was early evening here in Destiny, so it was almost one o'clock in the morning in France. "Why are you calling so late?"

"I understand you've been enjoying the fresh air and wide-open spaces of Wyoming for the last few weeks."

How did he know—

Other than her friend Lisa and her assistant at the foundation, both of whom she trusted implicitly, no one knew her precise location. "It wasn't part of my original itinerary, but yes, I am. How did you know where I was?"

"Technology is a wonderful thing, darling."

Priscilla's fingers tightened on her phone. She had no idea how he was tracking her, but if he was capable of making Jacqueline's antics disappear over the years—be it speeding tickets, underage drinking or even destruction of private property—of course he'd known where she'd been from the moment she'd fled.

"Now that you've reminded me of your far-reaching powers, I must go."

"Yes, your sister mentioned you were working on something. Are you putting your years of experience at the Lennox Foundation to good use?"

Yes, she was, and she was very proud of both her work with the auction and her work with the camp, but there was no way she was going to tell him— Wait, he'd actually spoken to Jacqueline? Suddenly, it all made sense. Paris was eight hours away from the French Riviera by car, ninety minutes by private jet. "What has she done now? No, please don't answer that. I don't have the time or the energy to deal with Jacqueline's latest exploit."

"Is that because of Jonathan?"

Tucking her phone between her shoulder and her ear, Priscilla looked down at her hands. Her nails were short, simply polished thanks to her most recent manicure at the local beauty shop, and her palms actually sported a few calluses from all her hard work at the camp. She hadn't thought about the ring Jonathan had given her, or the man it had represented, in the past several days. Not after she'd arranged for a private courier in Cheyenne to return the ring to the safety of a jeweler in Beverly Hills.

"No, it has nothing to do with him." Priscilla smiled, taking hold of the phone again. She marveled at how good it felt to say those words aloud, to feel that way deep inside. Her life was much better without her ex-boyfriend, but that didn't mean she wasn't still hurt by her sister's betrayal. "Jonathan is no longer part of my life. Nor is my sister, at least for the foreseeable future."

"Jacqueline has gone missing. She was last seen in Paris a few days ago. Alone. She was staying in one of our hotels, but never officially checked out."

The tight squeeze of her heart was so familiar Priscilla had to close her eyes. She had felt it many times over the years when it came to Jacqueline and her never-ending adventures. "That sounds just like her. You know how she comes and goes from the family's private suites all the time. She's probably found some mutual friends in the city and is staying with them."

"So you haven't heard from her?"

"We spoke on the phone three weeks ago. As you can imagine, it wasn't a very pleasant conversation."

"Very well. I'm sure you're right, but I'm going to get my people looking for her. Our family has been out of the spotlight for the last few weeks, and I want it to stay that way," her father said. "If you do hear from her, please let me know."

Priscilla agreed, pushing the niggle of worry from her mind and ending the call. As she walked back out into the main part of the bar, she thought about what she'd said to her father moments ago about Jonathan.

She hadn't loved him. She'd thought she did at one time, but she now realized Jonathan had fit the list of requirements she'd foolishly thought the right man for her needed to meet, if not exceed. When he'd hurt her by taking up with her sister, she'd blamed herself as much as she'd blamed them.

And what did it matter if only a few weeks, or even a few days, had gone by before she'd found herself in the arms of another man? Even if she'd been—what was that lovely phrase? Ah, yes. Smashed.

If she'd learned anything about herself over the past few weeks, it was to follow her instincts, not just in business, but in her personal life, as well. Instinct had told her to leave home when her world had turned upside down and that same inner voice had brought her here to this small town, to the camp and to Dean.

Why had she suddenly stopped trusting her own ability to make the right choices for herself? Was it because her stay here in Destiny was only temporary?

This time next week the auction would be over and there would be no reason for her to stick around. She'd still have a full month of her work sabbatical ahead of her and at this moment she had no idea where she was going next.

Maybe deep inside she'd been trying to protect her heart from getting too close to Dean. From being hurt again.

Still needing a bit more time to sort this out, Priscilla tucked her confusion over Dean away and joined her friends at the bar. The rehearsal was over and the bachelors were gone, as were most of the committee members.

"Do you think seven to ten minutes on average per bachelor is going to be enough time?" Racy asked, her hands filled with a giant wad of masking tape she'd just finished pulling off the dance floor. "What if we have a bidding war?"

Priscilla smiled at her concern as she retook her seat. "That's always a possibility, I guess. Of course, some of the bachelors might go even faster than we anticipate. If there isn't a lot of bidding going on for a particular man, we should declare the winner quickly, as we don't want to embarrass anyone."

"Which is why setting the minimum starting bid at fifty dollars was a good idea," Leeann said, joining them. "Even so, rumor has it the ladies of Destiny are planning to bid often and bid high."

"Let's keep our fingers crossed that there are no emergencies. We don't want our firemen or deputies abandoning us in the middle of the auction." Racy walked around the other side of the bar and deposited her trash.

An emergency was something Priscilla hadn't even thought about. What if for some reason Dean ended up not coming to the auction? Holly would be crushed. "I certainly hope no one gets called away that night, because we have someone who's already planning on spending her life savings on a bachelor."

At her friends' inquisitive looks, Priscilla explained about Holly and her plans to bid on Dean. Both Racy and Leeann came out with a collective "aww" and agreed the girl should be allowed to participate as long as Dean's date package was suitable for a younger bidder. In fact, they decided right then that Dean would be the last bachelor to go up for bid. Since the event flyers already stated only one bachelor per winner, Holly would have a better chance of achieving her goal.

"There wouldn't be any harm in letting as many ladies as we can know about the plan," Leeann said. "I figured Dean would go for a sizable amount, but wouldn't that be the sweetest way to end the evening, if they let her win?"

"I agree." An idea then came to her, and Priscilla added, "I'll talk with her mother tomorrow to make sure she's okay with her daughter's idea." And she'd confirm Holly had enough money to cover the minimum bid.

"We're going to have a packed house Friday night," Racy said. "Charging ten dollars per ticket just to attend the event is going to raise a lot of money, too. I know people are coming just to watch the festivities. My hubby included."

"Almost makes me wish Bobby was eligible to participate so I could bid on him." Leeann tilted her head and gazed at Priscilla. "Is that young camper getting in the way of any plans *you* had to bid?"

Despite what she had said that night to Dean's firefighting friends, Priscilla had to admit the idea of bidding on him had crossed her mind a few times in the past week. Not that it mattered now that Holly had shared her secret plan. There was no way Priscilla would try to take Dean away from her, but that didn't mean the two of them didn't have some unfinished business to take care of. Maybe they could find the time this week—

"Priscilla?"

The sound of a familiar male voice had Priscilla spinning around in her seat. "Oh, Dean! I didn't hear you—when did you get here?"

"Just now."

Priscilla looked around and found her friends had moved to the far end of the bar, giving the two of them as much privacy as they could expect in a place the size of the Blue Creek.

She turned back and found Dean had braced one arm on the bar and the other on the back of the barstool, trapping her with his body. That realization left her breathless. "You…you missed the rehearsal earlier this afternoon."

He nodded. "Bobby and I were working out at the camp."

She looked him over, taking in the dirty jeans, the sweat-dampened T-shirt and how his hair stood up in small tufts as if he'd recently run his fingers through it. "I can see that."

"I should've been here. I was…" He paused, his gaze dropping for a moment, but then he looked back into her eyes and said, "No excuses. I'm sorry."

A warm flutter started in her belly at the sincerity in his tone. "That's okay. We can walk you through what you need to do now—"

"What I need right now is to talk to you. Can you get away?"

Hadn't she just been thinking the same thing? Now that he was here, why was she suddenly reluctant to do so? "I don't know. The girls and I still have a few things to discuss."

He looked at her for a long moment. "Okay, we'll do this here. But in private."

He took a step back and held out a hand to help her down. She hesitated for a moment, but whatever he wanted to say must be important. *Trust your instincts, girl.* She placed her hand in his. His answering grin caused that flutter to become a tingling that raced through her entire body as he gave her hand a squeeze and led her through a swinging door and into a back hallway.

"We haven't had a chance to talk in the last week," he said.

This was actually the first time they'd been alone together since that morning she'd woken up hungover in his office. She'd missed talking to him, missed having him this close. "No, we haven't. I thought perhaps you skipped out on the rehearsal today because you had to go to Cheyenne again."

"No, I think my patient is finally in a good place, but you never know. Sometimes all it takes is a look, a word… or a kiss to knock a guy right on his ass."

The tingling vanished and her heart dropped to her stomach like a lead weight. The intensity of his stare told her that the guy he was talking about at this moment was him.

She owed him an explanation for her behavior that morning, that and more. "I'd hoped we could found some time to talk because I wanted to apologize for what happened… between us…down at the lake."

Dean's shoulders stiffened. "Apologize?"

"Yes. I know we were very much alone at the camp and the chances of anyone overhearing me asking for a kiss… of seeing you…seeing us…." Priscilla stopped to draw in a deep breath and realized her mistake as the move filled her head with the very masculine and outdoorsy scent of this man. Now she wanted to be the one to grab him and kiss him! "I never should've put you in that kind of situation. It was very unfair."

Dean moved forward and Priscilla instinctively backed up, deeper into the shadows, but the wall was there and before she could take another step, Dean flattened his hand on the surface next to her head. "Wait a minute. You were upset that morning because you were worried about me?"

"As you know, I had a lot to drink that night. Not that I planned it that way. I was just having so much fun. Something I haven't done in years on the chance that someone with a camera would be around if I said the wrong thing. Or did the wrong thing. I didn't want you to get caught up in that kind of madness." She was babbling and instinctively reached out, laying a hand on the center of Dean's chest. "Not that I think the kiss was wrong."

One corner of Dean's mouth rose into a slow smile. "No?"

"No!" Oh, she was saying this all wrong. "It's just that I've lived my life in the tabloids and it…sucks, for lack of a better word. Even the smallest thing can get blown out of proportion. Like that kiss. I know you thought it was no big deal, but—"

Dean lowered his head to nuzzle the side of her face. His lips, warm and soft at her hairline, moved to her cheek and then the spot where her ear and jaw met. "I lied. Kissing you was a very big deal."

Closing her eyes, Priscilla tilted her head, allowing him access to the curve of her neck. Her body hummed, his mouth on her skin causing her insides to awaken with a longing she'd never felt before. She pressed her fingers hard into his chest and his answering groan made her want to pull him close until the heat and hardness of his body was tight against hers.

"And I don't give a damn if anyone saw us, then or right now." His words were hypnotic and sinfully smooth, so much so that she hadn't realized he'd stopped kissing her until she felt the cool air on her skin. "But I know you do, so I'll behave. For now. How about you let me take you out for dinner tonight?"

She blinked and then opened her eyes, finding it hard to see past the intimate haze he'd just created around them. "Dinner? You mean like a date?"

Dean grinned and took a step back. "Yeah, a date. How about it?"

Before Priscilla could answer with a resounding yes, Leeann appeared, peeking around the swinging door. "Ah,

I hate to interrupt you two, but, Priscilla, I think you have a visitor out front."

Confused, Priscilla brushed past Dean when he took a step away from her. They walked back out into the bar, her gaze moving over several people milling around until one person caused her to do a double take. "Priscilla, darling!" A stunning brunette, poised with her arms flung wide in greeting, showed off her toned midriff in a cropped purple silk top. Completing the outfit were a pair of sleek black pants, strappy heels, a number of gold and beaded necklaces hanging around her neck and an oversize handbag that cost more than what one of Racy's waitresses could earn in a year of tips.

"Jacqueline." Her sister's name fell from her lips in an astounded whisper. "What in the hell are you doing here?"

Chapter Ten

"You barely let me say anything more than hello to your new friends before you dragged me out of there." Jacqueline pouted, tossed her purse aside and then threw herself down on the love seat in Priscilla's room at the inn. "But I must say, finding you in this little town, in the middle of Nowheresville, sitting on a barstool in a real country-and-western saloon—ohmigosh, too funny!"

Still in shock over the fact her sister was in Destiny, Priscilla followed Jacqueline into the room, placed her tote on the bed and then grabbed Snake's leash. The little guy was dancing around her feet, having barely given his true owner anything but a quick glance. Explanations would have to wait a few more minutes. "I need to take the dog outside. When I come back, I want some answers."

"I should've known you'd have Snaky with you." Jacqueline leaned down and wiggled her fingers, with their sparkly purple nails, at the dog, her voice suddenly childlike. "Come here, Snaky-poo, come see Mama."

Snake didn't budge an inch.

Priscilla rolled her eyes and attached the leash to the dog's collar. "Of course I have *Snake* with me. Did you think I would just leave him behind?"

"No, not you." Jacqueline's obstinate tone returned as she flopped back against the cushions. "Not the responsible Lennox daughter."

Priscilla had to bite down on her bottom lip to refrain from shooting back a retort of her own, but first things first. She'd take care of Snake and then get some answers from her sister.

The introductions back at the bar had been hasty, but the last thing she'd expected a few minutes after hearing Jacqueline was missing, not to mention moments away from making plans for the evening, was to see her sister walk into the Blue Creek Saloon as if she didn't have a care in the world.

And Dean…

She'd wanted to tell him how she'd intended to say yes, but he'd waved off his invitation with a whispered promise they'd do it another time. After that, Priscilla had hustled her sister out to the parking lot. On the ride back to the inn, with Jacqueline following close behind in a rented BMW, Priscilla had called her father to let him know Jacqueline had turned up.

Here. In Destiny.

Once downstairs, Priscilla stopped by the front desk to pick up a small trash bag and then took the pup to a wooded area out back to do his business. As much as she wanted to take the familiar walk through town that she and Snake did almost on a daily basis, Priscilla had to get back upstairs.

"Sorry, buddy." Priscilla entered the inn through the side door, depositing the bag in the designated receptacle and heading for the elevator. "I'll make it up to you, I promise."

Minutes later they were back in the room, with Snake giving a wide berth to Jacqueline as he made his way to his pillow near the fireplace. Slipping off her heels and her sweater, Priscilla sat in the chair opposite her sister, tucking her legs underneath her.

"Let's start with something simple. How did you get here?"

"A plane to New York and then another to Denver." Jacqueline crossed her legs, her foot bouncing madly. "Then I typed *Destiny, Wyoming*—great name for a town, by the way—into the navigation system of my rental and voilà, here I am."

"How did you know where to find me?"

"Daddy's secretary."

That answer shouldn't have surprised Priscilla. If her father knew her whereabouts, then Elizabeth would, too, and the woman had always had a soft spot for her sister. Jacqueline could always turn on the charm when needed, especially since making sure the transfer from Jacqueline's trust fund to her bank account every month was one of Elizabeth's jobs. "That's not exactly what I meant. How did you find me in town?"

"When I saw the choices for places to stay in town, I went with the B and B. I was heading here when I spotted your Mercedes in the saloon's parking lot."

"Do you know father is in Paris right now looking for you?"

Surprise crossed her sister's flawless complexion for a moment, before her sullen expression returned.

"Yes, the hotel staff called him," Priscilla continued. "They became concerned when they hadn't seen you—"

"And I bet you've already called him as well to tell him I'm here. We need to know where little Jacqueline is at all times, don't we?"

"Constant supervision wouldn't be needed if you would learn to—"

"I don't believe you!" Jacqueline jumped to her feet. "How can you sit there so cool and calm, like an ice princess? Aren't you going to ask me what I'm doing *here* instead of lounging on the beaches of the French Riviera? Or roaming the streets of Paris? Aren't you going to ask me about Jonathan?"

Priscilla fully expected some sort of visceral reaction to hearing her former beau's name, but there was nothing. No tightness in her chest, no loss of breath, no sharp pain in her gut. She was over him, truly and for good, but that didn't mean she hadn't been hurt by what her sister had done.

"No, I'm not. Jonathan is not my concern anymore." Priscilla looked intently at her sister, seeing the cracks in her spoiled-little-rich-girl facade for the first time. Something was wrong. "I'm assuming he's yours now."

"But he's not. Doesn't my being here make that abundantly clear?" Jacqueline paced around the room, her necklaces jangling as she moved. "We were having such a wonderful time together. Shopping, dining and dancing. He was so attentive, hanging on my every word, treating me like a queen.

"But then he woke up one morning, rolled over and announced he'd made a mistake—" she paused, a sob catching in her throat "—that being with me was a mistake. I didn't know what to say. I grabbed my stuff, threw it in a bag and was out of his penthouse before he got out of the shower."

Priscilla had no idea how to respond to her sister's outburst, so she remained silent. Not that her sister was stopping her rant long enough to give Priscilla a chance to speak.

"Thankfully, I ran into a friend who was heading to Paris, so I tagged along, and, of course, I went to one of our hotels. Drowning my sorrows with the finest champagne didn't do anything but make me sick. In the end I was still alone."

She stopped pacing and stood staring out through the window. "I was so…lost. I had no idea where to go or what to do. The one person that I could always turn to wasn't there—you. And I had no one to blame for that but myself."

Jacqueline turned and raced to Priscilla. Dropping to her knees, she buried her face in the folds of Priscilla's skirt. "I'm so sorry! What I did to you was terrible. I got so caught up in the moment I wasn't even thinking about the consequences of my actions. Of how it would affect you." Her words came out rushed and muffled. "I thought he loved me. I thought for the first time someone wanted to be with me…for me…but none of that matters. Even if any of that was true, it doesn't make it right. Oh, Sissy, please forgive me."

Stunned, Priscilla's hand hovered over her sister's dark hair for just a moment before she cupped Jacqueline's chin and gently lifted. The sight of her tears—real tears—reminded Priscilla of her own just three short weeks ago.

This was the first time she'd seen her sister cry since the day of their mother's funeral. In all these years Jacqueline had used many tricks to get out of whatever trouble she'd caused, but she'd never resorted to crying. Priscilla wondered if their father had given Jacqueline the same lecture about how the Lennox women weren't criers.

"I hurt you," Jacqueline whispered, "in a way that you probably can't forgive, but I want you to know I'm sorry. It's why I came here. I had to say it in person. I wish it had never happened."

"I wish it hadn't happened, either," Priscilla said. Her words weren't exactly the pardon her sister was looking for, but it was the best she could do at the moment.

Jacqueline wiped away her tears and launched herself into Priscilla's arms. Before she could even think about it, Priscilla embraced her sister and held her close, surprised to feel the bitter sting of tears behind her closed eyelids.

After a moment they separated and Jacqueline set back on her heels, a shaky smile on her face. "We haven't done that—hugged—in a very long time."

Priscilla nodded. "Yes, I know. So, what's next? When is your flight to Los Angeles?"

"I don't have a flight. I had no idea what was going to happen between us once we saw each other, but now I'm wondering…I'm thinking…maybe I could stay here with you? I would get my own room, of course, but there's nothing for me back home right now. And I need to take some time to think."

Once again Priscilla was surprised. Her first instinct was to say no, to get on her laptop and book a flight for her sister right now, even drive Jacqueline back to Denver herself. She didn't want anyone or anything to burst the perfect bubble she'd been living in the past couple of weeks. Working on the fund-raiser with the wonderful people of this town, being involved with Bobby and Leeann's summer camp, meeting Dean, spending time with him, kissing him…

"Priscilla?" Jacqueline tapped her on the knee. "What do you think? Maybe I could help with whatever project you're working on. Not that I have as much experience as you, but fund-raising is in our blood. Didn't I do an okay job of lining up the musical guest stars at the foundation's last fund-raiser?"

"But this is very low-key, just right for a town this size. It's more of a community event than a moneymaker."

"So what are you doing in a place that looks like a cross between Mayberry R. F. D. and the Wild West anyway?"

Jacqueline got to her feet and returned to sit down on the love seat, but this time she leaned forward, elbows on her knees. The tears were gone and a genuine smile was on her face. “Having a square dance?”

Priscilla pulled in a deep breath, sent up a silent prayer she was doing the right thing and said, “We’re doing a bachelor auction featuring local businessmen, cops, firemen, cowboys, et cetera.”

“A bachelor auction?” Jacqueline’s eyes lit up. “That sounds like an idea I would come up with. Wait! I did come up with that idea! How fun!”

“Yes, you did.” Priscilla smiled. “I hope you don’t mind I stole it from you.”

Jacqueline grinned and gave a dismissive wave. “After what I stole—nope, not going there. Don’t worry about it. Just tell me what I can do to help.”

On Monday morning Priscilla took Jacqueline to the auction committee meeting, after insisting her sister change her outfit twice before they left the inn. She’d explained how most in this small town dressed casually, if not a bit conservatively, and while she knew the arrival of her sister was news, Priscilla didn’t want to generate any unnecessary gossip.

Deep inside, she had to admit she’d been a bit nervous about Jacqueline being around Dean. Was it jealousy? Perhaps. Or maybe it was because he’d never asked about the quip she’d made about her sister and her ex that first day at the camp and so she’d never explained what had happened. She’d told herself it was none of his business, but she now realized that she hadn’t wanted anything from her previous life to invade what she had started to find in Destiny.

Allowing her sister to stay changed all that. Kissing Dean, wanting to out on a date with him, changed all that.

She wasn't sure how, or if it even mattered, but then Leeann had casually mentioned at the start of the meeting how Bobby and Dean had gone to Cheyenne to pick up supplies for the camp. Priscilla had tucked her disappointment at the news away, and now that the meeting was over, she was taking Jacqueline to see the camp. Much to their surprise, Snake had conceded to riding shotgun on her sister's lap.

When they arrived, Priscilla pulled into a spot behind the dining hall. They got out of her car and left Snake in the office with Leeann, who'd whispered to Priscilla she'd learned what Dean's date package was and that it would be perfect for Holly. She wanted to ask for details, but her sister was waiting. They spent the next hour or so walking around the camp as Priscilla gave her sister a personal tour. She introduced her to the staff they ran into and Jacqueline turned on the charm, flirting shamelessly when she met two of the camp counselors who were close to her age. The tour ended at the stables, and despite Jacqueline's inappropriate footwear, they managed a short trail ride with Holly and Alex, one of the counselors who also helped out around the stables.

"I need a few minutes to talk with someone," Priscilla said as she, Jacqueline and Holly headed back toward the dining hall. "Holly, would you please show my sister where she can get something to drink? I'll be back in just a few minutes."

Holly nodded, and Jacqueline, wiping the sweat from her brow, added, "Take your time. Don't worry about us. We'll find a nice shady spot to sit."

Moments later, Priscilla walked into the health center and found herself taking a quick peek inside Dean's office even though she knew he and Bobby still hadn't returned.

"Hey there, Priscilla. Are you looking for someone?"

She spun around. Holly's mother stood a few feet away.

"Yes, you. Do you have a few minutes to talk? It's about the bachelor auction. Holly said you two plan to attend."

"We sure do. Not that I'm looking to place a bid. Kevin might be on the other side of the world for the next five months, but I don't think he'd like the idea of me going out on a date." Bonnie sat down behind her desk and waved at a nearby chair. "Have a seat. What's up?"

Priscilla quickly explained about Holly's plan to bid on Dean and how she and the committee members hoped to make sure she had the winning bid.

Bonnie smiled. "That is so sweet of you all. Yes, my daughter has quite a fondness for Dean. It started on the very first day here at camp. Some of the other kids were teasing her and Dean came to her rescue."

"So you don't mind if she tries to win a date with him?"

"No, I don't mind. Holly is missing her dad very much. The two of them are so close. Kevin would often take her out, just the two of them, for dinner or to the movies. I know she's not trying to replace him…"

Priscilla swallowed back the lump in her throat when Bonnie's voice trailed off and she reached for a tissue.

"I guess my only concern is what Dean has planned for his date," Bonnie said. "Rumor has it some of the dates are very extravagant. Even romantic. Do you think we should tell him about this to make sure it's appropriate?"

Priscilla thought back to what Leeann had said earlier. She had to admit she was very curious, but she trusted Leeann's judgment. "I don't know what Dean has planned yet, but Leeann told me it'll be fine if Holly decides to go through with the bidding. Perhaps we should wait to say anything to Dean until Friday night, just in case she changes her mind at the last minute."

"Something my daughter has been known to do. A

woman's prerogative I guess, even if that woman is only nine years old."

They agreed to keep Holly's plan a secret for now, and Priscilla went back outside and started for the dining hall when she spotted the little girl walking toward her. "Hey there, what did you do with my sister?"

"I left her sitting on the back porch. She says her feet are killing her. I told her that her shoes are pretty, but all wrong for camp," Holly said. "I'm going over to see my mom now."

Priscilla grinned at the assessment and thought for a moment about asking her again if she was serious about bidding on Dean, but she figured Holly's mother would probably talk to her and there were still a few days before the auction. She would check with her one more time before then.

Her sister had disappeared again.

By Wednesday Jacqueline had become bored with Destiny and had started pestering Priscilla to head up to Jackson Hole. Jacqueline had found a world-class spa facility that was open year-round and she just had to visit. Priscilla had made it clear she couldn't leave town, not with the auction only two days away.

Not that she would admit it to her sister, but another reason she hadn't wanted to leave was that she still hadn't found the opportunity to spend time with Dean. They'd managed a quick hello on Tuesday afternoon before Jacqueline joined them, flirting with him the entire time they talked. This time the jealousy was quite real, an emotion so foreign to her—even after the whole Jonathan mess—that she had no idea how to deal with it. But there was no doubt the strain was back on their sisterly relations, as Priscilla felt compelled to keep Jacqueline under very close supervision. Then Dean had once again been called to the veterans' center and Priscilla hadn't seen or talked to him since.

Yesterday morning, the day before the auction, her sister had begged off going to the camp, claiming a headache, but by the time Priscilla returned later that afternoon, Jacqueline had left behind a note stating she was on her way to the spa and would be back in a couple of days. Priscilla had been livid over her sister's behavior, but by the time Jacqueline had left her a voice mail this morning saying she was in spa heaven, Priscilla had been too busy working out the final details for the auction to care.

Now, pacing backstage at the Blue Creek Saloon, Priscilla pushed aside any thoughts of her sister and concentrated once again on tonight's event. She was thankful for the headset she wore that, despite the noise, allowed her to communicate with Leeann, the girls manning the ticket booth and Racy, who was working upstairs with her sound and lighting people.

The bachelor auction had been going strong for just over two hours and the evening had been a rousing success. The place was packed, from the booths and tables to the rows of chairs that surrounded the runway. Everyone was having a wonderful time and from Priscilla's quick figuring, the winning bids for the bachelors were going on average from two hundred to four hundred dollars each. She was so proud of all the hard work that everyone had done to make this night go so perfectly.

Well, not quite perfectly, as they were two bachelors away from the end and Dean still hadn't made an appearance. But according to Bobby, who'd spoken to him earlier today, Dean promised he'd be here.

Making sure the microphone on her headset was set to mute, Priscilla peeked out from the side curtains, easily picking out Holly and her mother, who sat in the very front row on the right side of the runway. The little girl was determined to bid for Dean, and the plan was for Priscilla to join them just before he took the stage. Thanks to word-of-mouth among the bidders, the little camper was—fingers crossed—going to get her man.

"If he shows up." Dropping the curtain back in place, Priscilla leaned against the wall, hugging her leather portfolio to her chest. So far, Dean hadn't been seen in the building. In fact, he hadn't been in town for the past three days. "She will get her man if he shows up."

"You wouldn't be talking about me, would you?"

Priscilla spun around. There he was, looking impossibly handsome in a set of blue surgical scrubs that showed off his six-foot-plus frame to perfection. His hair was damp and he'd recently shaved. A clean outdoorsy scent clung to him that was so sexy Priscilla just stood there and stared.

"I can't believe..." Her throat tightened, but lifting her chin helped her to force the words out. "I'm so glad you could make it tonight."

"I said from the beginning I'd do this shindig of yours, right?"

Priscilla nodded. "Yes, you did. I hope your patient is okay."

Dean shrugged and for a moment it looked as if he had the weight of the world on his shoulders. "We thought he was...okay. He was saying the right things and doing the right things, but then his life got complicated. Again. I'm just glad I was there when he needed me.

"Not that this is what I planned to wear tonight—" he grinned, attempting to lighten his mood as he gestured to himself "—but it was the only clean outfit I had with me in Cheyenne. I grabbed a quick shower, changed and drove straight here."

"You look good." Boy, did he ever. "The outfit, I mean. It's fine."

Dean's gaze darkened as he looked down at her. "You look pretty fine yourself."

Priscilla blushed under his heated gaze. "Thank you."

"I guess our crazy schedules haven't allowed us to spend much time together, huh?"

"I'm so sorry. I really wanted to accept your invite—"

He moved in close and pressed a finger to her lips for a moment, rendering her speechless, before he dropped his hand away. "No more apologies. We'll find time for that date, okay?"

Priscilla nodded, hoping he was right.

"So, where's that sister of yours?" He backed up a step and looked around the backstage area. "I figured she'd be working alongside you tonight."

Jacqueline was the last thing Priscilla wanted to talk about right now, especially with Dean. "Oh, I'm sure she's out somewhere causing havoc and having fun."

He turned back to her, confusion crossing his features. "I don't understand. Are you mad at her? I mean, I know you have the right to be mad at her. At least, I think you do. But I was under the impression the two of you had worked out your problems."

"If you're referring to my ex-boyfriend, yes, the problem has been resolved. In fact, he and I were done and over with a long time ago. It just took me a while to see it."

His mouth curved into a devastating smile. "That's good to hear."

"But Jacqueline is…well, she's her own unique person. It's hard to know exactly what she's— What I mean is, I'm not sure she's ever going to— Oh, enough about her." Priscilla casually waved her hand as if it was that easy to dismiss her sister. It wasn't, but she was determined not to let Jacqueline spoil this. "So, you're the last bachelor of the evening and you're on next. This is your spot here, and then the curtains will open—"

"Look, before I go out there, I want you to know I had my doubts about this whole crazy idea in the beginning. When I found out you were from Beverly Hills and what kind of events you've done in the past, I'll admit I was worried tonight might turn into…I don't know, something outrageous and over-the-top. A circuslike atmosphere that didn't fit the small town of Destiny or its people." Dean's smile went from devastating to sheepish and back again. "When I'm wrong, I say I'm wrong."

Priscilla basked in his approval, enjoying the warmth she saw in his gaze. Dean started to say something else but she raised a finger, signaling her need for silence as she listened to Leeann masterfully handle the bidding for the gentleman who was on stage, just as she'd done all night long. Loud applause filled the air, signaling his time on stage was coming to an end.

Priscilla decided right then that Dean deserved to know about Holly's plan to bid on him. It wasn't fair to have him walk out on that stage and find out no one would be trying to win him except for one little girl. "Listen, it's almost time for you to go on, but there's something I have to tell you."

"Is it about my date package?" Dean asked. "I know starting the evening with an early dinner out at the winner's choice of one of the local restaurants isn't very creative but I hoped the horse-drawn carriage would be considered a nice added touch."

"No, that's not what I was going to say, but that sounds… wonderful."

And magical and perfect. Priscilla had decided not to find out what Dean's package would be. She would just be surprised when she heard it for the first time tonight, and quite honestly she didn't want to know what she'd be missing out on, as there was no way she would bid against Holly.

Now she knew. A carriage ride with Dean.

"Priscilla, are you there?" Racy's voice filled her earpiece. "Can you hear me? I think we got a situation out here."

Priscilla thumbed the microphone. "What kind of situation?"

"Your sister has just made a grand entrance and now she's making her way through the crowd. And she's not alone."

Priscilla's heart sank to her stomach. "What do you mean Jacqueline's not alone?"

The noise level from out front grew even louder and Racy had to raise her voice to be heard. "You better come out and see for yourself."

Priscilla pushed past Dean and headed for the front of the stage, but he was right next to her. They moved to the curtained area behind the podium where Leeann was standing and looked out into the bar.

Priscilla couldn't believe her eyes. Hopeless bewilderment rushed through her before it morphed into a smoldering anger.

There stood her sister on the edge of the dance floor, draped in a floor-length fur coat of all things, despite it being a hot July evening. The two men with her looked very familiar even though Priscilla had no idea who they were or where they came from. One was a photographer, his flash going off like Fourth of July sparklers as he aimed his camera around the room. The other was operating a handheld recording device, his in-your-face attitude telling Priscilla he was a reporter.

Jacqueline had returned and she'd brought the paparazzi with her.

Chapter Eleven

"What the hell is going on?" The chaos raging out in the main area of the Blue Creek Saloon had Dean turning to Priscilla. "What is your sister doing? Holding a press conference?"

Priscilla sighed and took a step back, releasing the curtain. "I have no idea what Jacqueline is up to. She left town a couple of days ago—"

"Left town? When I spoke with her on Tuesday all she could talk about was the auction. How excited she was to be helping you and all these great ideas she had."

"Yes, well, my sister has been known to change her mind…rapidly. She'd talked about going to a spa in Jackson Hole. How she got there…how she got back…and why those people are with her—"

"Are you telling me you didn't plan this? That this isn't some publicity stunt cooked up by the two of you—"

"No! Of course not! The editor from Destiny's local weekly paper is here to do a story, but not this!"

He wanted to believe her. He'd meant what he said about his concerns over how tonight would turn out. In the back of his mind, he'd wondered if Priscilla would try to pull something out of her Beverly Hills lifestyle, like bring in a big-name bachelor celebrity or who knew what else, but he'd seen how hard she'd worked to keep the auction low-key and focused on the town and their support of the camp.

The paleness of her features told him she was upset at what her sister was doing out there, but she didn't seem completely surprised by it. "Did you expect her to pull a stunt like this?"

"Nothing my sister does surprises me anymore."

Dean rubbed at his jaw, suddenly wishing he'd grabbed a cold beer before coming backstage. "Well, what are we going to do now?"

Priscilla turned away and put a hand to her ear as she spoke into her headset. He couldn't make out her words, but then she looked back at him and said, "You're going to get out there on that stage and we are going to finish this auction. I'll take care of this."

Before Dean could say another word, she whirled around and stomped away, putting one determined, sexy high heel in front of the other. And damn if he didn't take a moment to admire how the little black dress she wore showed off her toned arms and legs to perfection. Her hair was down, the golden waves loose and flowing around her shoulders. A quick inhale filled his head with her fresh, summery perfume even after she had disappeared from view.

Dean had hoped to get here early enough tonight to talk to her, maybe even set a date for dinner, but that would have to wait, especially now. At least he'd been glad to hear her assertion that things were finished with her ex-boyfriend. One less thing to worry about, but he still wasn't clear as to exactly why her sister had suddenly shown up in town.

And why she was out there acting like a starlet at a red-carpet premiere.

Something about the whole setup put him on edge, reminding him how far removed Priscilla's world was from his, no matter how well she seemed to be fitting in. Hell, he'd almost…

Nolan Murphy, the oldest of the Murphy brothers and the architect who'd designed Camp Diamond, walked past, yanking off his tie. "What a mess. I'm glad that's over. Of course, Liam's not going to let me forget he got a higher bid then me. And my kids aren't going to be happy when they find out I'm going on a date with the high-school vice principal." He gave Dean a light punch in the arm. "Hey, Zip, wake up. You're on."

Dean saw two elderly women, regulars at the weekly bingo night, waving frantically at him as they held open the center curtain. He joined them, and seconds later they shoved him out onto the stage, their hands precariously close to his backside. A spotlight hit him square in the chest as Leeann's voice filled the air.

"And, ladies, here he is…Destiny's last bachelor! Let's hear it for Dean Zippenella!"

Loud applause and a few whistles and catcalls filled the air, but Dean still managed to hear a loud whisper coming from one of the ladies behind him.

"Move that cute butt of yours down the runway. Pronto."

He obeyed, and the cheers grew louder as Leeann continued reading his bio.

"Dean is a transplant to our fine little town—all the way from the shores of New Jersey—but you'd never know it with the way he has fit right into Destiny. He's dressed tonight in those dashing medical scrubs, à la Dr. McDreamy, because he just got off work as a physical therapist at the veterans' center in Cheyenne. A former decorated soldier, he works with our brave military men and women who have been injured in service to our country. He's also one of our newest volunteer firefighters and was instrumental in the design and creation of Camp Diamond, the reason we're all here tonight."

Dean had to admit he felt a little silly as he made his way down the runway. He smiled and waved, but the spotlight shining in his eyes made it difficult for him to see anything, including if Priscilla had gone to talk to her sister. He certainly hoped so. He'd gotten the impression when he arrived tonight that the evening was a big success. The last thing he wanted was for something, or someone, to turn things ugly.

"The lucky winner will enjoy dinner at a restaurant of her choice in town, and she'll arrive in style, as Dean has secured the use of a restored American buckboard buggy that will be pulled by a gleaming white horse. After dinner, there will be a beautiful ride in the countryside to Winchester Farm and a sunset hot-air-balloon ride—"

"That's enough—we're sold!" a feminine voice called out from Dean's left. "Let's start the bidding!"

The swell of applause from the crowd showed they agreed as bursts of lights came from numerous cameras. By the time Dean made it to the end of the runway, he found himself wondering what Priscilla thought of his date package. When he'd mentioned the horse-drawn carriage backstage, her eyes had lit up and her smile had softened. He knew how much she liked horses, which was why he'd chosen to include the carriage ride as part of his package.

She'd said before she wasn't going to bid on any of the bachelors tonight, but would she stick to her word? Would she perhaps bid on him? They certainly had a lot to talk about.

"Okay." Leeann's voice once again came over the sound

system. "As you know, ladies, those of you who have already won a date this evening aren't allowed to bid again. Our minimum bid for each bachelor is fifty dollars.... Do we have any opening bids?"

"I bid fifty dollars."

Dean jerked his head, looking over his right shoulder at the row of ladies sitting there. Why did that voice sound familiar? And why did it sound so young? Almost like a kid's voice? Thankfully, the spotlight was gone and the house lights were raised a bit, making it easier for him to see out into the crowd. Before he could zero in on the bidder, another feminine voice filled the air.

"Fifty bucks? Oh, we can't let such a hunky prize go for such a measly amount."

Dean looked back toward the end of the runway, easily spotting Priscilla's sister, who stood right in front of him with a cocktail in one hand and a numbered paddle in the other. She raised her glass at him in a salute and the flash from the photographer filled the air with more bursts of light.

"I bid five hundred dollars."

Five hundred dollars? What was her sister thinking?

Priscilla had come out from the backstage area and tried to get to Jacqueline, but the place was just too crowded, and too many people had stopped her, wanting to talk. As soon as Dean had stepped out from behind the curtains, Priscilla made her way to where Holly sat with her mother, just as she had promised. She'd hoped Jacqueline didn't have any other stupid antics up her sleeve.

She'd been wrong.

A collective gasp had gone out from the crowd at her sister's outrageous bid. Only one of the other bachelors tonight had gone for more than that amount—Liam Murphy and his helicopter ride to Jackson Hole, of all places, had been won for the grand total of six hundred and twenty-five dollars.

"What does that mean, Mommy?"

Priscilla looked down at Holly and then at Bonnie, reading the confusion on the little girl's face and the disappointment on her mother's.

"Remember when I explained to you how an auction works?" Bonnie asked her daughter. "Whichever person bids the highest amount wins."

"But I only had ninety-two dollars and thirty eight cents in my piggy bank," Holly said, before looking down at the tiny purse in her lap. "I guess that means I won't get to go for the buggy ride or the balloon ride with Mr. Dean."

Priscilla clenched her hands tightly in her lap, wanting nothing more than to get ahold of her sister and shake some sense into her. It was bad enough she'd shown up with members of the press in her back pocket, but to place a bid? At the moment, Priscilla couldn't remember if she'd ever told Jacqueline about Holly and Dean and the plan to let the young girl win the auction. Not that it mattered. Deep inside, Priscilla knew her sister would've gone ahead and placed the extravagant bid anyway.

"We have a very generous bid of five hundred dollars for our last bachelor." Leeann spoke into the microphone, but when Priscilla looked up, she found Leeann looking right at her. "Do we have any other bids?"

Priscilla reached for Holly's hand and gave it a quick squeeze. "Let's get you that date."

Holly nodded with enthusiasm, but it was her mother who spoke. "You don't have to do this. That's a lot of money."

Yes, she did. Yanking off her headset, Priscilla held

out her hand to the young girl, who grinned up at her and quickly placed her bidding paddle in Priscilla's palm.

Priscilla raised the paddle into the air and called out, "Six hundred dollars."

The crowd started cheering again, but all Priscilla could focus on was the shocked look on Dean's face as he stared back at her. Then she stole a glimpse at Jacqueline, who had one hand on her hip and the other one curled around the glass at her lips.

Six fifty. Jacqueline mouthed the amount, knowing full well no one could hear her, but Priscilla had been able to easily read her sister's lips.

Did she think this was some sort of game? There was no way her sister could know all that had happened between her and Dean over the past month. If she did, she wouldn't be doing this now. Not after the remorse she'd shown over her involvement with Priscilla's ex. Priscilla desperately wanted to believe that, but deep inside she just wasn't sure. She shook her head in warning. Would it work?

"Six fifty," Jacqueline repeated, this time loud enough to be heard above the noisy crowd.

Priscilla stood. "Seven fifty."

"Eight fifty."

A hush settled over the room except for a few muted whispers here and there. Priscilla could only guess the townspeople were trying to figure out who these two strangers were that were battling for a date with one of their own. And bidding such crazy amounts. Although most people probably recognized her from the past month she'd spent in Destiny, Priscilla was still an outsider. An outsider who was determined not to let her spoiled sister have her way.

An outsider who wanted to make a little girl happy.

Priscilla glanced up at Dean again, who stood there,

arms crossed over his chest, not looking very happy with the bidding war that was going on. She would explain everything to him. After she won.

"One thousand dollars." She gripped the bidding paddle tightly in her hand. There was no need to raise it in the air. Not with everyone in the room staring at her and Jacqueline.

"Heck, for that amount of money, Dean can go out with both of them," a man called out from somewhere deep in the crowd and everyone laughed.

Everyone except Dean.

"How about it?" Jacqueline move forward a few steps, the photographer and the reporter on her heels. "You ready to take on the Lennox sisters? Twelve hundred and fifty dollars."

The revelation that these two women were siblings carried through the crowd like a storm cloud racing across a leaded sky. Mortified at being the center of attention, Priscilla struggled not to meet anyone's direct stare, but in the process her gaze clashed with Dean's again and held for a long moment.

He then turned away. Dropping his arms, he held them out as if he was surrendering and addressed the crowd. "I don't know about taking on the two of them. I might not have the strength."

Laughter filled the air.

"Hey, you better make sure she likes dogs, Zippenella. Or should it be that your dog likes her?"

Dean laughed along with everyone else, but Priscilla had heard his husky chuckle often enough in the past month to easily deduce it was forced this time.

"Well, we all know that Daisy has gotten better at making friends lately thanks to Miss Lennox." Dean turned and gestured at Priscilla. "What's that song about sisters? You know, how they think and act as one?"

The laughter and applause was loud again, but Priscilla could hear in Dean's voice that he hadn't been teasing. Did he really believe what he'd said? It didn't matter. She had to end this and it had to be now.

"Two thousand dollars." The laughter faded enough so that Priscilla could easily hear Dean swearing under his breath about her high bid, but she kept her gaze on Leeann, willing her to finalize things and put them out of their misery.

"We have a bid of two thousand dollars. Going once… going twice…" Leeann paused, as was the standard practice, but when silence filled the air she banged her gavel on the podium. "Gone!"

A cheer rose from the crowd as everyone got to their feet, applauding. "Ladies and gentlemen, this concludes our auction," Leeann continued, her voice strong as she spoke into the microphone. "Bobby and I would like to thank everyone for your generous contributions to Camp Diamond. Please stay and enjoy yourselves for the rest of the evening."

The noise level in the bar grew even louder as the crowd began to disperse. Priscilla released the breath she hadn't even realized she'd been holding and then was grabbed around the waist in a pint-size hug.

"Oh, thank you, thank you! I can't believe you did that for me."

Priscilla dropped to her knees and returned Holly's exuberant hug. "You're most welcome, sweetie. I'm sure you'll have a good time with Mr. Dean."

"Can I tell him how excited I am? And ask him when we're going to have our date?"

Priscilla looked up at Holly's mother. "Maybe I should explain things first—"

"You can talk to Dean another time," Bonnie said to her daughter. "Besides, it's Saturday morning where your daddy is and we don't want to miss our video chat with him, do we?"

Getting to her feet, Priscilla gave Bonnie a quick hug and whispered, "Thank you. I want to explain everything to Dean before Holly talks to him."

"It's me who should be thanking you. The amount of money you spent—"

"It's all going to a very worthy cause." Priscilla waved off Maggie's gratitude and then watched as the two gathered their things and disappeared into the crowd.

She should find her sister and corral her before she caused any more trouble tonight, but she had to talk to Dean first. Looking around, she tried to find him, but there were too many people. Then she spotted him near the far-stage area. It took her a few moments, but she finally reached him.

"Dean." She put a hand on his arm to get his attention. The tightness of his muscles and his jerky movements spoke volumes of his mood. "Dean, please, I need to speak with you."

He didn't even look up from where he was stacking the metal folding chairs onto a rolling cart. "I think you've said enough tonight."

"I want to explain what happened."

"I know exactly what happened. I was the tennis ball in some sort of back-and-forth game of one-upmanship you and your sister were playing." Another four chairs joined the growing pile. "Congratulations, sweetheart. You won the prize."

Priscilla's heart ached at his tone, but he had every right to be angry with her. Perhaps when she explained why she had done it… "You don't understand. *I* didn't win anything."

"Thanks a lot."

She shook her head at his sarcastic tone. "That's not what I meant. I don't want you to take me out—"

Dean turned to face her. "Too bad. The whole town knows you won me tonight. We're going to have that date whether either one of us wants it or not."

"Dean—"

"Are you busy this Sunday?"

His question confused her. "Sunday? No, I don't think so, but—"

"Good. Leeann didn't get a chance to mention it, but decent weather is required for the carriage and the balloon ride. I've made arrangements to have both on Sunday evening. I have on-site duty this weekend at the veterans' center, but I'll be back in time to pick you up around five. Dress casual."

Priscilla looked around, noticing they were starting to get some unwanted attention, including that of the photographer. "If I could just talk to you privately, please?"

"Oh, if I'd known private time was included, I would've bid more. Much more."

Jacqueline's voice flowed over Priscilla's shoulder and Dean narrowed his gaze, the dusky brown of his eyes going even darker. He opened his mouth to speak, but then pressed it closed and said nothing as he went back to work on clearing the chairs.

Priscilla spun around and came face-to-face with her sister. And her entourage. Ignoring the flashes from the photographer's camera, she sank her fingers into the thick, furry pelt of Jacqueline's coat, pulling her away from Dean. "What were you thinking?"

"Just having a little bit of fun and supporting a local charity." Jacqueline yanked free from her hold. "Not as much fun as you're going to have, of course."

Priscilla looked closely at her sister, this time noticing

the glazed expression in her eyes. The strong smell of alcohol on Jacqueline's breath had her taking a step back.

"Hey, listen, these guys are going to do a story about you." Her sister waved a hand at the two men standing next to her. "And the camp and the auction. You might want to talk to them."

Priscilla sighed. Talking with a reporter was the last thing she wanted to do, but she had enough experience with these people to know if she didn't tell her side of the story, they'd print what they'd learned from other sources, namely her sister. Still, she looked back over her shoulder, suddenly thinking perhaps Dean could sit in on the discussion to talk about the camp, but he had disappeared into the crowd. "Fine. I'll talk to them, but not here and not now."

"We need to do this soon, Miss Lennox." The reporter stepped forward. "My editor wants me to file the story as soon as possible."

"May I ask what outlet you're with?"

"The *Jackson Hole Star.* It's a weekly magazine. I met your sister at the Mountaintop Resort and Spa, and when she mentioned what you were doing here in this small town—"

"Yes, of course, but I still have things I need to finalize here concerning the auction."

"They're staying at the inn. Isn't that convenient?" Jacqueline said with a tight smile. "You can talk to them when you get back to your room."

The headache that had threatened from the moment her sister had shown up tonight finally fractured into a thousand pieces when Priscilla walked into her room at the inn. Snake greeted her from the comfort of his pillow with the rapid beating of his tiny tail.

"It's always nice to have someone happy to see you, isn't it, buddy?"

She kicked off her shoes and placed the cashbox from the auction on the bed. She'd kept it with her since leaving the bar, but now that she was back here for the night, she was thankful there was a safe in the room where she could lock up the cash, personal checks and credit-card receipts. When all was said and done, they'd raised more than ten thousand dollars for the camp.

Priscilla got a water bottle from the tiny refrigerator and quickly downed two aspirin, fearing they weren't going to help very much. The headache had started during the half hour she'd spent in the front parlor talking with the two people from the magazine. She'd used her years of experience to downplay her sister's involvement in the auction and steer the reporters away from pursuing the story angle that the two sisters were fish out of water slumming it so far from Beverly Hills. She'd tried to keep the focus on the camp and the wonderful work Bobby and Leeann were doing as owners, suggesting the reporters contact them to be interviewed, as well.

Thankfully, according to Minnie Gates, her sister had already gone up to her own room by the time Priscilla returned, but she still had no idea how and why Jacqueline had gotten those reporters to the auction.

And she wasn't waiting until tomorrow morning to find out.

She retrieved her cell phone from her purse and dialed Jacqueline's number. While she waited for her sister to answer, Priscilla looked at her dog. "Fair warning, she's coming over."

Snake jumped off his pillow, grabbed it with his teeth and dragged it into the bathroom. Priscilla couldn't blame him one bit.

"I guess you want to talk to me now." Jacqueline's voice didn't sound quite so animated when she finally answered. Perhaps her liquid courage was wearing off. "Is the queen requesting my presence?"

Priscilla rolled her eyes, but only said, "Would you please come over?"

"Your wish is my command."

Tossing her phone on the bed, Priscilla stripped out of her dress and slipped into a pair of leggings and a baggy T-shirt just as Jacqueline knocked on the door. Priscilla let her in, noticing the elaborate makeup had been washed away. Jacqueline had pulled her hair back into a ponytail and wore a similar outfit.

Determined not to be swayed at how young her sister looked, Priscilla motioned for her to take a seat. Then she remembered the cashbox and turned back to the bed.

"Do we really have to do this tonight? I'm tired."

Grabbing the box, Priscilla opened the oversize armoire and knelt in front of the safe. "Yes, we *really* have to do this tonight. What in the world were you thinking when you showed up at the auction and caused such a...disturbance?"

Silence filled the air. Priscilla leaned back and looked over at the love seat to make sure her sister was still awake. She was—in fact, she was staring at Priscilla with an almost stricken expression on her face.

"What? What's wrong?"

Jacqueline blinked hard and shook her head, as if she was waking up from a trance. "Nothing. Other than my usual lack of decorum and manners."

Priscilla went back, entering the four-digit code to ensure the safe was locked. She stood again, closed the armoire door and joined her sister. It was hard to believe it had only been five days since they had sat in these very same positions while Jacqueline poured her heart out. Priscilla had wanted so much to believe in the sincerity of her sister's words, but now…

"I asked you to come over so I could find out why you bid on Dean tonight."

"Oh, are we a bit jealous? Don't be. You won."

Priscilla decided it wasn't worth the effort to explain the connection to Holly, but she did make a mental note to get in touch with Holly's mother tomorrow to make sure that Sunday was okay for Holly's date with Dean. She also had to get ahold of him to explain what he wouldn't let her say tonight. His earlier words of praise filled her head, including how he'd initially been worried she'd somehow turn tonight into something overblown and dramatic but then came to trust her. Did he believe her when she'd told him she had nothing to do with her sister's antics?

Focusing her thoughts, she looked at Jacqueline and asked, "Why did you leave town without telling me? And why did you bring those reporters back with you?"

Jacqueline grabbed one of the small pillows and hugged it to her chest. "You know why I left. I was bored. I wanted something to do. You might think this small town is a little slice of paradise, but it's not to me."

"If you were having such a fabulous time—shopping and being pampered at the spa—why did you come back so soon?"

Jacqueline mumbled under her breath but all Priscilla could make out was something about being cut off.

"What did you say?" she asked.

"I'm broke!" Jacqueline tossed the pillow onto the empty chair nearby. "I was asked to leave the resort because Daddy canceled my credit cards. He also blocked access to my trust fund. I had to find a way to pay the bill at the hotel, so when I met those reporters in the bar, I sold them the story about you, this big-shot Beverly Hills philanthropist spending her summer in a backwoods, Podunk town raising money for a kids' summer camp. When they found out the auction was tonight, they paid my bill and offered me a ride back down here."

Priscilla couldn't believe it. Their father had finally taken a hard-line stance against Jacqueline's irresponsible and immature behavior, but Priscilla was the one who was paying the price. Again. A month ago her world had been turned upside down, but the idea that anyone in Destiny could be hurt by what was going to be printed was so much worse. Destiny was a good place. These were good people. They didn't deserve the backlash that something like this could create, especially if the wire news services picked up on the story. And because of her last name, they probably would.

She closed her eyes, willing back the sting of tears. To find such a wonderful place and to lose it in such a short amount of time, Priscilla suddenly felt as lost as she had the day she pulled into town.

"Priscilla? Are you okay?"

"You have more important things to be worried about than me." She opened her eyes and looked at her sister. "What are you going to do now?"

Jacqueline seemed surprised by the simple question. "I... don't know. I thought maybe you could help—"

"You're on your own." It was so easy to say the words, Priscilla wondered why it had taken so long for her to do so. "It's time to grow up, Jacqueline. Own up to your mistakes. Make things right."

"Are you serious?"

"Very. I'm guessing you can't pay your bill here at the inn?"

Her sister started to say something, but then snapped her mouth shut and just shook her head.

"I thought not. Fine, your room was booked for a week. You'll be checking out on Monday, but I don't want to hear a peep out of you—and you know exactly what I mean by that—until you leave town."

"So what happens on Monday? That's only a few days away." Jacqueline got to her feet, annoyance coloring her features. "I've only got a couple of hundred dollars in my wallet."

"Then I suggest you either call Father or find the closest bus terminal."

Chapter Twelve

Dean sat at the bar, nursing his beer, enjoying the peace and quiet of the small hole-in-the-wall tavern on the other side of town from the Blue Creek Saloon. There were only half a dozen or so people here, most of them twice his age, as the clientele who came here were mostly older cowboys and ranchers. There was no dance floor, no menu. Just a jukebox and a scattering of tables.

Someone slid onto the barstool to his right, but Dean didn't recognize the man as they exchanged a nod in greeting and then went back to minding their own business.

"I thought you had to go back down to the veterans' center."

Now, that was a voice Dean recognized. He turned as Bobby sat down. "I don't have to report in until eight o'clock tomorrow morning. What are you doing here? I thought you were taking your wife home."

"I did." Bobby gestured to the bartender to bring him the same as what Dean was drinking. "After we got home, she told me to find you. Thought you could use a friend. I spotted your truck as I was heading back to the Blue Creek."

Dean snorted. "Actually, I was looking for solitude."

"Looking to drown your sorrows?"

"What sorrows?" Dean took a long draw from his beer and swallowed. "Just because the guys at the firehouse will keep what happened tonight alive for months? Or maybe if I'm real lucky, my picture will show up in the newspaper. Either way I've got a date with the lady who paid a lot of money to spend an evening with me, even if she doesn't want to."

"Did she come right out and say that? Didn't you two talk afterward?"

Dean flashed back to when Priscilla found him after the auction had ended. It didn't make any sense. She wanted to go out with him. She'd said as much said backstage before the crazy bidding war with her sister. Why was she backing out now? "She tried, but I wasn't in the mood to listen."

"Then maybe you just need to trust her."

Dean exhaled loudly. "Why? What aren't you telling me?"

"I just think…well, considering how much Priscilla paid for your company, I'd say otherwise."

"Then you'd be wrong. She was just trying to outdo her sister. But I'm not really surprised. I guess that's how Beverly Hills socialites get on in the world. With wads of cash. High society and a small town like Destiny do not mix well."

"What in the heck do you mean by that?"

"Look back to when we first met. That woman was standoffish and wound tighter than that antique grandfather clock at your place. Walking around in her fancy dresses and high heels—"

"And looking damn good while doing so, you have to admit."

Okay, Dean would give her that. "Yes, she did, but every word that came out of her mouth sounded like it was painted with twenty-four-karat gold—"

"She was a stranger in a strange place," Bobby interrupted. "I remember a certain Jersey boy who had a bit of a hard time when he first came out West."

Dean laughed, silently admitting his friend was right about that, too. "Yeah, well, it didn't take me long to get into the swing of things."

"It hasn't taken Priscilla too long, either. She's been here, what, a month, and look how well she's gotten along with everyone."

"Thanks to that crazy bachelor-auction idea."

"An idea everybody in this town supported from the beginning, even you, with a little arm-twisting from my wife."

"It didn't take the city long to track her down, though, did it? I had a feeling something like this might happen." Dean thought back to his initial concerns about the auction that first day on Bobby's back deck. "That she would somehow find a way to turn tonight into a circus."

"Are you sure you're not thinking about someone else?" Bobby asked. "Someone who once tried to use your connections to skirt the law?"

Dean took another long draw on his beer. As the cold liquid flowed down his throat, he realized his first instinct had been to shoot down his buddy's question, but he'd be lying. There were times he found himself comparing Priscilla to his last steady relationship, even though he knew it wasn't fair. They were two different women and he was far from the same guy he'd been three years ago.

Maybe because he'd fallen hard for Katherine the first time he'd seen her and ignored the warning signs they were incompatible. Signs that had been so clear once the relationship ended. After seeing her true colors, he'd vowed not to be blindsided by a woman ever again. Everyone had their faults, him included, but was he purposely looking for liabilities in Priscilla that weren't there?

"You can't lay that on Priscilla. I only met her sister a couple of times this week, but she seemed like an okay kid. I know Priscilla wasn't happy when she found out she'd taken off yesterday. Not that she said anything, but I got the feeling that making tracks is a habit of Jacqueline's."

That was the third time Bobby had been right and it was getting annoying. Priscilla had seemed genuinely upset with her sister, both backstage and during the bidding process. And if there was anybody who knew about the craziness of sibling relationships, it was him.

"And I've got to say she did jump right in and get her hands dirty at the camp," Dean admitted. "From everything you've told me about what went on while I was gone, and everything I've seen for myself, she's done an amazing job with the kids."

"And *for* the kids," he continued. "The auction tonight was a big success, despite the madness at the very end. Everybody had a great time, from the bachelors to the audience. It was exactly the kind of event Leeann and I wanted."

Dean nodded in agreement.

"And you've got to admit one more thing." Bobby leaned over and tapped the long neck of his beer bottle against Dean's. "That mutt of yours does think that girl is something pretty special."

Dean laughed and felt his bitterness over the night's events fade. "Too bad that rat she calls a pet doesn't feel the same way about me."

"Maybe Snake isn't sure about you because he knows you're not sure about Priscilla. Yet."

That was the problem: he'd thought he was, especially after that moment at the Blue Creek when he'd asked her out to dinner, but tonight raised old doubts. But how much of that was actually her fault? Probably not much, if he were honest with himself. He should have stuck around to hear her out but instead he'd run. And now it might be too late. Ever since that night down by the lake, Dean's feelings for a woman he'd only known a few short weeks were growing and finding a way deep into his heart. At the moment, he didn't have any idea where those feelings might lead. And after tonight he was worried that the answer was nowhere. Unless he could somehow fix things.

It took Dean longer than he'd planned to get to the Painted Lady Inn on Sunday afternoon to pick up Priscilla for their date. Probably because Sam Winchester, the owner of the rig, had insisted on giving Dean another lesson in handling the buggy and the horse.

But he was finally here.

And according to the voice mail he'd just listened to, he was actually taking out Holly Warren, that cute kid from the camp, tonight.

What was going on?

Dean climbed down and handed the reins off to the Major, who was waiting in the parking lot. "Would you mind keeping an eye on her while I see if my date's ready?"

"Will do."

Heading inside, Dean waved to Minnie and then got into the elevator. A few minutes later he was standing outside of Priscilla's room. He knocked and an instant later she answered, wearing a pair of shorts and a T-shirt, her feet bare.

He leaned against the doorframe, going for relaxed because damned if she didn't look completely sexy. "I know I said casual, but isn't this a little too casual?"

"You're here." She took a step forward and closed the door behind her. "Please tell me you got my messages."

"The last one. Are you backing out on me?"

Priscilla laid a hand on his arm, her fingers cool on his skin. "I've been trying to tell you since the night of the auction—this date was never for me."

What was she talking about? "Are you serious? I'm taking out—"

The door flew open and there stood Holly, all dressed up in her Sunday best. "Hi, Mr. Dean! Are you here to pick me up for our date? I'm so excited!"

Priscilla moved in close, her back to the room and her voice barely above a whisper. "As soon as Holly heard about the auction, she wanted to place a bid. On you. That was always the plan."

Dean just stood there, his gaze going from the young girl to her mother, who stood behind her, and then back to the girl again. It took him a few seconds to process what Priscilla has just said, but then he put it all together. He couldn't believe how wrong he had been about her true motives that night.

"Yes, of course I'm here for you," he finally said to Holly, stepping into the room as he pushed the words past the lump in his throat. "And don't you look pretty."

Holly beamed, but her mother must've picked up on Dean's initial confusion because she said, "Sweetie, why don't we go into the bathroom and check your hair one more time?" She then sent a smile in Dean and Priscilla's direction. "We'll be right back."

Dean waited until the door was closed before he turned to Priscilla, who was cradling Snake in her hands. "I know this is going to sound crazy, but please tell me the Warrens didn't pay two thousand dollars for tonight," he said. "All she had to do was ask. I would've done this for nothing."

Priscilla smiled. "Why didn't I think of that instead of spending my hard-earned money to win you…for her?"

Now it all made sense, including the cryptic answers Bobby had given him in the bar. He must've known about this, too. "So that's what happened Friday? That's what you were trying to tell me?"

"As soon as I learned of Holly's plan, all the ladies on the committee worked hard behind the scenes to make sure that she would win." She moved past him and put Snake down on top of the same pillow Dean had hunted down a couple of weeks ago. "Her mother, of course, agreed with the idea, telling us how much Holly misses her dad and the special one-on-one time they'd often spend together. Not that you can take her father's place, but we thought… well, you must be aware that she has quite a case of hero worship for you."

Dean felt his face go hot as he eyed the dog, a part of him wondering what the animal was going to do next. But Snake only returned his stare for a moment and then circled twice before curling up in a ball and closing his eyes.

"Dean? Did you hear me?"

"Yeah…sure, I noticed. It's kind of hard to miss."

"She had a little over ninety dollars saved up, and that's what you would've gone for. If my sister hadn't stepped in and caused all that trouble."

Dean wondered if her sister was still in town, but that wasn't important right now. "If *you* hadn't stepped in to make sure that little girl got what she wanted."

Priscilla lifted her shoulders in a delicate shrug as she walked past him to the window. "I know what it's like to have a wish."

So did he. Dean walked up behind her and waited as she pulled the curtain to one side and looked down into the parking lot where the horse and buggy stood waiting.

"Oh, Dean…a white horse." Her voice dropped to a whisper.

The lump in his throat grew. "Wishes are important. No matter how long it takes for them to come true."

Priscilla turned back around to face him and Dean wanted nothing more than to pull her into his arms and kiss her. But a soft click told him the bathroom door was opening and his date was coming back out.

Priscilla grabbed a small white box off the corner of her desk and pressed it into his hand. "It's a corsage for Holly. Trust me, all girls love flowers."

Dean took the box and presented it to the very excited little girl with a great flourish while Priscilla and her mother looked on. Then the four of them went downstairs and joined the crowd that had gathered outside around the carriage. Dean introduced Holly to the horse, then gently lifted her into the carriage and sat there as Bonnie—and quite a few other people—took pictures. Then he grabbed the horse's reins and they started off down Main Street.

"So where would you like to go for dinner?" he asked the young girl sitting next to him.

"Sherry's Diner," Holly answered without hesitation. "They have the best hamburgers and chocolate milk shakes in town."

Dean bent down and gently nudged her shoulder with his own. "You're my kind of date."

It was just after 9:00 p.m. when Dean pulled his truck to a stop in front of the inn and shut down the engine. He thought back to what his parents had always said about how nobody needed to call someone after nine o'clock at night unless it was an emergency.

Looking up, he was relieved to find the light still on

in Priscilla's room. No, this wasn't an emergency, but he couldn't wait one more minute to see her again.

He got out of his truck and walked up the front steps of the inn. Entering the foyer, he spotted the Major sitting behind the front desk.

"Making a late-night call on one of my guests, soldier?"

Dean smiled. "Yes, sir."

"Carry on."

Resisting the urge to salute, Dean got into the elevator. When he arrived at Priscilla's door, he took a deep breath and knocked. He heard her moving inside the room and he suddenly wondered if perhaps her sister was in there, too. Just when he thought he should go back downstairs and use the housephone to call her room, the door opened.

Every ounce of air left his body.

Priscilla stood in front of him looking like an angel. Her hair was just the way he liked it, loose and flowing around her shoulders, and she wore a white silky robe that belted at her waist. The deep V where the two sides came together at her breasts was edged with lace that didn't quite conceal the creamy perfection of her skin. As his gaze dipped lower, he found her bare toes peeking out from the edge of the material and he immediately wondered if she were naked beneath her robe.

And if he'd gotten her out of bed.

"Dean, what a surprise."

"I know it's kind of late…"

"No, it's not." She opened the door wider. "Please, come in."

Dean started to do as she instructed, but stopped short when her dog popped around the corner of the couch. Snake had been, if not nice, at least tolerant of him being here earlier, but that didn't mean he'd welcome him a second time. "Are you sure it's okay?"

Priscilla looked confused for a moment until she spotted the dog. "Oh, don't worry about him. Snake was probably just making sure you weren't my sister. Don't worry, buddy. Jacqueline is already in bed for the night next door."

Dean stepped into the room and closed the door behind him. "So, you're not too crazy about Jacqueline either, huh," he said to the dog directly. "Looks like you and I have finally found some common ground."

Priscilla and Dean both laughed as Snake seemed to nod his head before he went back for his pillow, this time burrowing inside what looked like a miniature sleeping bag until the only thing visible was his tail.

"Does he always sleep like that?" Dean asked.

Priscilla nodded, looking at her dog. "It's strange, but it works for him."

"Lucky you. Daisy shares my bed. Lately she's taken a fancy to my pillow."

Priscilla laughed again and then moved into the sitting area of the large room, taking a seat on one end of the small couch. "How did things go with Holly?"

Dean smiled. "We had a good time. We went to Sherry's for dinner, a place her and her dad visit often when he's home. She really got a kick out of the buggy ride, and when that hot-air balloon left the ground, I don't think I've ever heard a kid squeal so loud. But in a good way."

"I'm sure she'll remember this evening for the rest of her life."

He hoped so. He'd put in a standing order for the entire Warren family to take a balloon ride once Kevin got home. Not to mention he planned another buggy ride in the near future with the pretty lady in front of him.

"I don't mean to be presumptuous, but are those for me?"

Dean looked down at the flowers in his hand. How could he have forgotten about them after he'd lucked out and found the owner of the local flower shop working late tonight? He thrust them at her. "Yes, of course."

She stood again and took them, her fingers grazing his. "They're so beautiful. Thank you. Let me find something to put them in."

Dean moved to one side as she walked past and disappeared into the bathroom. His gaze followed her as she passed the four-poster bed and the only light in the room, which was coming from the bedside lamp. The blankets were pushed back on one side, a paperback book lying near the pillows, and an awareness that she *had* been in bed caused his body to tighten. He was glad he'd worn his shirt untucked. Just the same, he sat down as she came back out into the room carrying the flowers in a vase.

Priscilla crossed the room and set the flowers on the desk in front of the windows. Her fingers lightly moved over the individual buds before she pulled a single yellow rose free and lifted it to her cheek, brushing it against her skin. "You didn't have to do this, but thank you again."

"Yes, I did. Like you said when you gave me Holly's corsage, all girls love flowers. Besides, my *nonni* always told me that when a man is going to apologize he should bring flowers."

She smiled and joined him on the couch, bringing the rose with her. "Your grandmother's a very wise woman. But no apology is needed."

"That's where you're wrong." Dean shifted closer and took her hand. "I am sorry for the way I treated you at the auction. I didn't know what was going on, and instead of listening to you, I was a stubborn jerk. I should've trusted that you knew what you were doing, just like you've done ever since you've been here."

Priscilla's fingers curled around his. "Well, I wouldn't say that. There have been many times in the last few weeks that I had no idea what I was doing."

"Not when it came to the auction."

"Even then. I'd never done a fund-raiser like that before, and I'm not just talking about the smaller scale." Priscilla smiled and brought the rose to her lips. "And I was certainly at a loss when it came to knowing my way around the camp."

"Except for the stables," Dean said, determined to make her see all the good she had done in the short amount of time she'd been in Destiny. "And it didn't take you long to find a way to leave your mark on Camp Diamond with all your great ideas. You've made it a better place, Priscilla. I'm sorry if I ever did anything to make you doubt that."

Priscilla stared at him, her blue eyes wide, and it was all he could do to keep from reaching for her. Desire clawed at him, urgent and hot and sharp. His jeans were suddenly too tight and even the cotton material of his button-down shirt felt too restrictive. He brushed his thumb back and forth across the ridge of her knuckles before he finally gave in and brought her hand to his lips.

"Dean…"

His gaze locked with hers as he placed a kiss on the back of her hand. He then gave a gentle tug and suddenly she was there in his arms. Pulling her up hard against his chest, his hands slid over the cool silkiness of her robe. Her arms encircled his shoulders, her hands caressing the back of his head as their lips met. He leaned back against the couch, dragging her into his lap as he kissed her with all the pent-up emotions from the past two weeks.

This was what he'd wanted from the moment that first kiss had ended. Hell, this was what he'd wanted from the moment he'd first seen her. Their mouths were demanding and greedy, their kisses hungry and breathless. He finally released her, but only so he could trail his lips down her neck and across her collarbone. She tipped her head back, granting him access, and he took it as one hand encircled her waist while the other rode low on her hip and pressed her even harder to him.

His lips found the curve of her breast at the same moment his hand moved to the knot of her belt. He found himself wanting to ask permission, but then Priscilla's delicate fingers covered his and she tugged at the material. In one smooth motion, her robe parted and he slipped his hand inside, something erupting within him as his thumb scraped across her hardened nipple.

Her breath exited on a moan as she pressed herself into his touch.

Yes. This.

She did a little shimmy with her shoulders, and the robe floated down and away from her shoulders, catching in the crooks of her arms.

He took a moment to stare at how unbelievably beautiful she was, before giving in to what his body craved. Groaning, he drew her breast into his mouth, a heady sense of relief filling him as she directed him, her fingers tunneling deep into his hair.

He finally lifted his head, watching her face as he whispered, "I want you, Priscilla. I want to make love to you."

She slowly rose from his lap until she stood directly in front of him. When she reached for her robe, a sinking feeling filled his gut. Then he realized she was loosening the belt completely, and seconds later the material slid to the floor and she stood before him gloriously naked and utterly perfect.

She held out her hand and Dean grasped it with his as he tried to stand. Not an easy thing for a man in his condition to do. A soft giggle escaped her lips as she made quick work of the buttons on his shirt and seconds later released the top button at the waistband of his jeans.

"Is that better?" she asked in a soft whisper.

Despite the need still pulsing through his body, he loved the humor he saw shining in her eyes. "You have no idea."

"Well, cowboy, you still have on more clothes than I do."

"I think that's a problem we can take care of quickly."

He picked her up, enjoying her squeal of surprise as he carried her over to the bed. As he laid her down, she pushed her book to the floor and then scooted beneath the covers. She watched him undress, her smile turning brazen when he pulled a trio of condom packets from his back pocket and laid them on the bedside table. "Feeling ambitious?"

"You have no idea."

"Well, then, let's put that ambition to work." She then beckoned him with a simple curling of her finger and welcomed him home.

The morning sun streamed through the lace curtains, causing Priscilla to stretch as she tried to wake up, but the heavy weight of an arm around her waist, not to mention the wall of muscle pressing against her from her shoulders to her backside, reminded her that she hadn't slept alone last night.

"Good morning," Dean's deep voice murmured in her ear, sending a wave of shivers across her naked skin. "Sleep well?"

Priscilla smiled. She had, even though it had been for only a few hours. They had made love through the night, and in between talked and laughed and shared stories of everything from their childhoods and romantic pasts to Dean and Holly's adventures, until Priscilla had finally closed her eyes. And yes, they'd used all three of those condoms. "I could always use more beauty sleep."

Dean's arm tightened around her, pulling her close before he placed a whiskery kiss on her shoulder. "Says who?"

Her heart swelled, overflowing with emotions that she couldn't label or at least didn't want to yet. She'd been overwhelmed with the way Dean had responded to the surprise that Holly was his date yesterday evening. And while she'd admitted to a wee bit of jealousy as the two of them rode off in the horse-drawn carriage, it had been the tears in Bonnie's eyes as she talked about emailing the photos she'd taken to her husband in Afghanistan that made Priscilla realize that all the madness on Friday night had been worth it.

"Hey, I can feel the wheels turning in your head," Dean said. "What are you thinking about?"

Priscilla smiled and wiggled her hips, loving the rumble of laughter from deep in his chest.

"Forget it. I don't have the strength."

"Is that a challenge?" she asked.

"No, it's a fact. Hey, what time is it?" Dean rolled away from her toward the alarm clock on his side of the bed. He groaned and said, "Damn, it's almost seven o'clock. Don't hate me, but I've got to get going."

Priscilla turned to face him, holding the sheet to her breasts. "Do you really?" Had that come out sounding as desperate as she thought? "I mean, of course not. I don't hate you. It is, after all, Monday morning."

"That it is. Hey, I've got a few in-home visits to do around town this morning. I should be done close to noontime. How about I pick us up some lunch at Doucette's Bakery and meet you back here?"

Priscilla smiled, that mushy emotion she refused to label returning. "Sounds wonderful."

"It's a date." Dean leaned forward and pressed a quick

kiss to her nose. He then sat up, threw his legs over the side of the bed and froze. "Umm, hello."

Priscilla rose up on one hip and scooted behind him, letting out a laugh when she spotted Snake looking up at them as he sat on the pile of clothing that belonged to Dean. "Well, look at it this way. He didn't pee on them or chew them up."

"Very funny." Dean reached back with one hand, tunneling his fingers into her hair and bringing her face to his for another kiss, this time on the lips. "Is he going to give up his spot so I can get dressed?"

"He probably has to go outside." Priscilla moved back to her side of the bed and got out from beneath the covers. "I guess I'm getting dressed, too."

She walked over to the sitting area and picked up her robe from the floor where she'd dropped it last night. She slipped it on and then turned around to find Dean standing next to the bed, tugging his jeans up over his hips, a sly grin on his face while he watched her.

"I certainly hope you're wearing more than that when you take him out," he said. "Or you might find yourself flat on your back again, despite my weakened condition."

"Just give me a minute to put on some clothes and the two of us will walk you to your truck."

A flicker of an emotion she couldn't read danced over his features, but then he turned away and pulled on his shirt. "Okay."

Five minutes later they were outside, with Dean insisting he had time to walk into the woods with her and Snake. When they were done, he ushered her back to the side entrance of the inn and pulled her into his strong embrace, his face buried in her hair, his mouth at her ear.

"Last night was incredible." His words were soft, but

they ignited a fire deep within her. "I'm glad I ignored my inner demon and came over."

"What does that make me? One of your better angels?"

"You *are* an angel." He pressed his lips to her ear and then to her neck. "Now get back inside. I'll see you later."

Refusing to allow any doubt to get in the way of her happiness, Priscilla was downright giddy as she and Snake headed to her room. She took a shower, unable to stop thinking about where things might be headed with Dean as she stood beneath the hot spray. Was it just a fling? No, it was more than that. At least for her. And she still had another month before her leave of absence was over and she had to make a decision about her next step.

Could that step be one that took her away from Beverly Hills altogether?

The camp still needed more funds, more promotion. The auction had been fun. While support from the town was important and a yearly event of some sort could be done, she still believed her plan to bring in wealthy individual supporters was the best way to secure long-term funding for the camp. It only made sense for her to work on that right here in Destiny, which meant more time with her new friends and with Dean. Of course, she needed to clear her plans with Bobby and Leeann, but they had been on board with her ideas from the beginning.

She got out of the shower, dressed and thought about breakfast, but the dining room wouldn't be open for another hour. Her gaze caught on the safe in the bottom of the armoire. Deciding to create a spreadsheet of the auction receipts, she removed the cashbox and walked to the desk.

Strange she hadn't heard from Jacqueline yet. Oh, well. Her sister normally slept late.

While waiting for her laptop to power up, she opened the box and a sudden coldness washed over her. She reached out with shaking fingers to tunnel through the paperwork, personal checks and credit-cards receipts, but deep inside she knew what her eyes refused to believe.

The cash was gone.

Chapter Thirteen

Priscilla scraped at her eyes, the tears making it hard for her to see as she drove back from Laramie to the inn. She'd been at the local branch of her bank when it opened and, after waiting through an interminably long computer glitch, withdrawn the necessary amount to replace the $4,800 missing from the cashbox.

After discovering the money was gone, she'd immediately raced to find Jacqueline, even though she'd known the room would be empty. Repeated phone calls had gone unanswered. Priscilla had then tried her father's secretary, who said she hadn't heard from Jacqueline since last Friday and, of course, her father was in a business meeting and couldn't be disturbed.

Despite her recent vow not to play rescuer anymore, Priscilla had to replace the missing cash before anyone found out. She'd calculated the amount needed and left for Laramie, all the while trying to figure out how Jacqueline had managed to get access to the money. Priscilla had gone over the contents of the cashbox on Saturday, but then hadn't touched it again until this morning. She had been at the camp most of the weekend as they had welcomed a new group of campers, and she and her sister had actually had dinner together Saturday night.

She was sure Jacqueline had come up with some reason for Minnie, or whoever had been manning the front desk, to allow her into Priscilla's room when she was away, but there was a four-digit security code that opened the safe.

However she'd pulled it off, Jacqueline wasn't going to get away with this. Priscilla would eventually find her sister and deal with her for this unthinkable act, but she refused to allow all the hard work of everyone involved with the auction to be tainted by her sister's immature behavior.

And if she was being honest, she had to admit that the idea of revealing what Jacqueline had done to anyone—especially to Dean—shattered her heart. Just a couple of hours ago she'd been daydreaming about what the future might hold for the two of them....

She refused to think about that now. Minutes later, she jumped out of her car after returning to the inn and raced upstairs to her room.

Dean stood at the counter of the bakery and realized he had no idea what kind of sandwich Priscilla would like for lunch. He always got the Doucette Deli Special, loaded with four different kinds of meat, cheese, some veggies and a spicy sauce that had quite a kick. He supposed they could split the sandwich, but then he spotted the Tanya Veggie, a healthy vegetarian option, and decided to go with that.

"Welcome to Doucette's. How can I help you?"

Dean placed his order with the teenager behind the counter, paid for it and then stepped aside to wait. The bakery was busy, but he found a quiet corner and started to think about the same thing that had been on his mind all morning.

Priscilla.

Things were moving pretty fast between them and he had no idea what was going to happen next.

If anyone knew he was thinking this way, they'd laugh. Dean had to admit he'd dated—and slept with—a good number of women since moving to Destiny, despite how much Daisy hampered his social life. He'd always made sure that every lady he got involved with was aware from the very beginning that he had no interest in settling down. A determination he had made after things with his ex had ended so badly.

The mantra had been working for him, but ever since he woke up today—no, from the moment he'd made love to her the first time last night—something had changed in him. When she'd gotten out of bed this morning and casually walked across the room to retrieve her robe, he'd had a sudden vision in his head of watching her do that every morning for the rest of his life.

And, yeah, it had freaked him out. So much so that he'd decided he needed to get away to think for a while.

How could things be moving this fast? Hell, they hadn't even gone on a real date yet. He wanted to take her on a carriage ride, dance with her at the Blue Creek Saloon, be by her side as she experienced her first rodeo, share the beauty of a Wyoming sunset from the front porch of his log home and watch her awaken in the morning as the sunrise shone through the oversize window that filled one wall of his bedroom....

Now that the auction was over, would he have the chance to do any of those things with her? Despite her being on what she called a sabbatical from her job in L.A., he figured she planned to return home eventually. Would she ever be willing to leave that ritzy life behind for a much quieter one here in Destiny? Was he crazy enough to think that the past four weeks—and one night of great sex—were enough to build a future on?

"Excuse me, Dean. Can I speak with you for a minute?"

Dean turned and found Jill Doucette, one of the owners of the bakery, standing there. "Sure, Jill. What's up?"

She backed up through a door that led into the kitchen and motioned for him to follow her. He did, right into the tiny office, noticing she held something rolled up in her hands.

"We got these in this morning." Jill unfurled what turned out to be a magazine. "They're not supposed to go on display until tomorrow, but when I opened the box..."

There were three images on the glossy cover of the *Jackson Star*: one of him dressed in scrubs on stage during the auction, one of Priscilla and him in a heated argument, and a last shot of Jacqueline, posing in her fur coat with a drink in one hand in a bidding paddle in the other. The headline read "Hollywood Heiress Saves Summer Camp and Heals Heart?"

He let out a colorful expletive that would've had his mother and his *nonni* cuffing him upside the head. He had no idea the reporters Priscilla's sister had brought to the auction that night were connected to this gossip rag. He yanked open the cover and quickly scanned the article, his shock turning to outrage at how Priscilla was portrayed as a martyr who'd come to town and single-handedly saved Camp Diamond after being dumped by her millionaire boyfriend.

Priscilla had told him all that had gone on with her sister and her ex-boyfriend, including how Jacqueline had ended up here in town, during the wee hours of the morning, so none of that was a surprise. Hell, she'd told him how she, with her father's connections, had been cleaning up Jacqueline's messes for years. Funny how neither one of them had even thought about how this latest fiasco of her sister's would turn out when the article was published. They'd had been too distracted, or unwilling, to think too far outside of what was happening right there in Priscilla's bed.

As he continued reading, Dean's stomach flipped over and then crashed to his feet when he found he was quoted in the article as well, and it wasn't good. Or the truth. Some of the phrasing sounded familiar, and he racked his brain trying to figure out how—

Friday night. After the auction. The stranger who'd sat beside him when he and Bobby talked must've been a reporter. Dammit!

He looked at Jill and read sympathy in her gaze. "My folks and I have decided not to display this issue, but White's Liquors and the general store carry it, as well. My mom's already headed to both places to talk to them…." Her voice trailed off and she shrugged, silently telling him that there was no way to stop the article from being seen, as the magazine was probably available statewide.

An employee interrupted them, Dean's order in his hands. He took it, even though his appetite was gone, thanked Jill profusely and hurried from the store. His only thought was to get to Priscilla before someone else showed her this garbage.

When he got to the inn, he was glad to see Priscilla's car in the parking lot. Having no idea how he was going to tell her, Dean shoved the magazine into the bag of food and went inside. As he headed toward her room, he noticed the door was ajar. What the—

He rapped hard with his knuckles, pushed it open and stepped inside. "Priscilla? Are you here?"

"Oh!" The shriek fell from her lips as she whipped

around, nearly falling from where she sat perched on the edge of the bed. "Dean!"

"Sorry if I scared you," he said, ignoring the wild beating of his own heart. "Your door was open and I got worried there for second."

He placed the food on a nearby table and then noticed the large amount of money in her hands and a cashbox on the bed. Latching on to any excuse to put off talking about the magazine for the moment, he said, "Is that the take from the bachelor auction? You never told me the final tally. Can I help you count?"

"No, that's okay—" Her voice cracked and Priscilla crushed the bills to her chest. "I don't need any help. I'll finish this later." She cleared her throat and turned away, but not before Dean had seen the redness in her eyes and the bright patches on her cheeks.

His heart sank as he glanced back at the food. Had she already seen the article? Had she read it? Did she think he had actually said those things?

"Is there a reason why you've been crying?"

"I'm not…crying. I just don't feel very well." She pulled in a deep breath and a shudder caused her shoulders to quiver. "Can we please do lunch another time?"

If she thought he was just going to walk away, she had a thing or two to learn about him. "I can't leave you like this."

"Like what?" Priscilla's voice rose. "I'm fine. Please… I just want to—"

Dean sat on the bed next to her. "Something's wrong. Tell me."

His weight caused the mattress to shift and the cashbox toppled to the floor, its top springing open and the contents falling out. "Ah, hell. Sorry about that."

Dropping to his knees, Dean began gathering the personal checks, credit-card receipts and a large amount of cash. Confused, he looked up and found Priscilla staring at him, astonishment on her face.

He glanced back and forth between the cash in his hand and the money she still held in hers. "I don't get it. What's with the two piles of money? Were you planning to match the funds that were raised?"

The money was back.

The fear and dread that had been churning inside of Priscilla reached a fever pitch when Dean walked into her room moments ago, but now it morphed into elation when she saw the cash lying on the floor among the paperwork. Tears filled her eyes again. Somehow during the hour and a half it had taken her to get down to Laramie, get the replacement funds and return, Jacqueline had come back and replaced what she had taken to the cashbox that Priscilla had left lying on her bed.

"Can you explain this?"

Priscilla brushed the wetness from her cheeks, remembering the large amount of money she held in her own hands. She looked down at it, realizing Dean's assumption would be a perfect excuse to describe what was going on, but she couldn't do it. She couldn't lie to him.

Pulling in a deep breath, she slowly released it and decided to start at the beginning. "Well, I went to count the receipts this morning—"

"And discovered your sister had stolen the cash?"

Priscilla gasped and then saw the handwritten note Dean held in his hand.

"'Please forgive me.'" Dean's mocking tone stung as he flipped the card around and read her sister's words. "'I don't know what I was thinking. It's all here. Love, Jacqueline.'"

Priscilla's head spun. "I—I can't believe she did that."

"I can't believe you were going to cover for her."

Priscilla stared at him, not surprised that he'd figured it out so quickly. "I know replacing the cash was a knee-jerk reaction—"

"Ya think?" Dean got to his feet, shoving the paperwork and the money back inside the box. "I would've thought the last month had cured you of that."

Priscilla stood, her back now ramrod straight. She shuffled the bills in her hand into a neat pile before shoving them back into a nearby envelope. "I've been taking care of my sister pretty much since she was eight years old. It's not a switch I can turn off so easily."

Dean tossed the box onto the bed. "Since your mother died. Yes, you told me stories last night about how you saved her ass time and time again, but this is different. You can't use your money or your position in society to change the fact that she broke the law and you're letting her get away with it."

"The money is back. No crime actually took place." It was a fine line, but not one she was willing to cross. At least not yet. "There's no reason to tell anyone about this." She shuddered at the thought of what the press would do with this—the press! Oh, no! How had she completely forgotten about those reporters at the auction Friday night? She'd been so caught up in dealing with her sister, the camp, getting Holly ready and then last night with Dean…

"Except maybe the sheriff?"

Closing her eyes, Priscilla drew in a deep breath. "You talked about your family, too. About their rich history in law enforcement. I know how you must feel about something like this—"

"You have no idea."

"Jacqueline is my sister. I know what she did was wrong. Very wrong and it can't be excused. But I made the decision to make things right in the best way possible for everyone."

Judging by the way Dean stood there, feet planted apart and arms crossed over his chest, it didn't matter what she said. They stared at each other, silence filling the air as neither one was willing to bend. Then, just for a moment, she thought she'd seen a hint of empathy or kindness in his eyes before he blinked and it disappeared.

"Are you planning on telling someone about what happened?" she asked.

"No. But not because I don't think I should."

There was another long beat of silence.

"I better go," he whispered, his voice miserable.

Priscilla clenched her hands to her stomach, wanting so much to cross the small space between them and fling her arms around him, but experience and the unofficial Lennox family motto of keeping emotions in check in front of others kept her rooted to her spot except for a brief nod. "That would probably be best."

Dean turned around and walked out.

She stood there for moment longer, trying to convince herself that not running after him was the right thing to do. It was then she noticed the paper sack he'd left on the table. She turned away, but her gaze landed on the four-poster bed. Had only a few hours passed since she'd awakened warm and safe in Dean's arms as they talked and made plans for lunch?

Eating was the last thing she wanted to do right now, so she grabbed the bag and walked over to the small refrigerator. At the sound of the door opening, Snake appeared at her side. "Taking refuge in the bathroom again, huh? You are one smart dog."

She gave him a treat and then placed the two sandwiches and the bottled waters inside the refrigerator before her hand caught on something inside the bag.

Pulling out a magazine, she sucked in a shallow breath.

It was a tabloid! Those reporters her sister had brought to the auction had been from a celebrity tabloid!

For the second time in less than thirty days, Priscilla Lennox found herself featured in a clever headline that was only a prelude to what she was sure was a scintillating article inside. Unlike the first time, when she'd never bothered to look for the published report online, Priscilla flipped open the magazine and began to read.

Her knees buckled before she got through the first few paragraphs. When she got to the unnamed female source quoted as saying Priscilla had showed these country bumpkins a thing or two about putting on a fund-raiser, she collapsed to the carpet.

Snake whimpered and crawled into her lap. Priscilla petted him, certain her aching heart couldn't take much more. She almost stopped reading, but then found a quote attributed to an unnamed male that could only be Dean as he described her high heels and twenty-four-karat words.

She tossed the magazine aside. It was only a matter of time before everyone in town read this article, and while most intelligent adults knew the difference between tabloid journalism and the real stuff, there were many who would believe it. As much as she hated to admit it, portions of what was written did have a ring of truth.

She was an outsider. She didn't belong here and others obviously felt the same way. It was time for this fairy tale to come to an end. Still, she sat in that very spot for hours, waiting to see if her sister would return. Finally, she decided to pack her bags.

The sun was setting when she checked out of the inn, securing the cashbox in the main safe located in the office downstairs. Leaving like this, without telling anyone, was a cowardly thing to do. She tried to justify it by telling herself that she should be gone before word of the magazine article got around town.

"Are you sure you're okay to drive?" Minnie asked as she gave Priscilla a hug goodbye. "You seem a bit upset, dear."

"I'm fine. I just need to return to L.A. to deal with some unexpected family business." Priscilla tugged on Snake's, leash as the dog proved reluctant to leave the inn's front porch. "Please thank the Major for me. I loved spending time here."

It was hard to believe after all the crying she'd done today that she had any tears left, but when the sharp sting reached the back of her eyes, Priscilla scooped Snake into her arms, hurried to her car and headed for the West Coast.

The pounding on Dean's front door matched the pounding inside his head, and Daisy's barking didn't help. He stumbled from his couch and blindly made his way to the foyer, almost tripping over his dog before yanking open the door.

Bobby stood there waving something in his hand, but Dean's blurred vision, combined with the morning sun, made it impossible for him to see anything clearly.

"What?" he croaked. "What are you doing here so early?"

Bobby pushed past him and came inside. At least that meant Dean could close the door. He did so and then turned around, finding himself face-to-face with his best friend.

"Are you crazy?"

Bobby shoved something at him and Dean grabbed at it, but missed. The object landed on the floor with a light thump, and then he saw his own image staring back at him and realized it was that gossip rag. The sudden pain in his chest was worse than the headache slamming around in his brain. "Where in the hell did you get that?"

"I take it from your question you already know about that piece of crap. You want to explain?"

Talking was the last thing Dean wanted to do, but the look on his buddy's face told him that arguing would only be a waste of breath. He pushed past Bobby and headed for the kitchen. Pouring two cups of coffee, he thanked whoever invented programmable coffeemakers, and downed two mouthfuls. Then Bobby entered the room with Daisy close behind, the magazine held tight in her jaw.

Dean had realized a few hours after their argument that he'd never talked to Priscilla about the article. He'd tried to call her a few times, if for no other reason than to make sure she knew the truth about what he'd said—and hadn't said—but he'd never even reached her voice mail on her cell phone.

Bobby grabbed the second mug and then said, "Since you seem to be having a hard time getting your mouth moving this morning, I'll start. Priscilla left town last night."

Stumbling backward, Dean landed on one of his barstools. He grabbed at the wooden seat with one hand, praying it would anchor his suddenly spinning world. The news was the last thing he'd expected, even after everything that had happened yesterday.

"Leeann and I woke up this morning to an email sent around midnight that said she had an emergency in L.A. and she apologized for leaving so abruptly. The fact she included attachments of all of her fund-raising plans for the camp leads us to believe she's not coming back anytime soon. If ever." Bobby gestured with his coffee cup to the magazine, which Daisy was in the process of tearing up into tiny little pieces. "And I think that article, and you, have more to do with her being gone than anything else."

Bobby's words left him feeling hollow. Dean explained everything that had happened in the past couple of days, including how the money had disappeared and then reappeared. By the time he was done, he felt better despite his raging hangover.

"That's all you've got?" Bobby gave a disgusted sigh. "You need to fix this."

"Really? That's the only advice *you've* got?"

"You're in love with this woman, Zip. Do I have to say that aloud? Fine, I'll tell you again and maybe it'll sink into your thick skull. You. Love. Her. You need her in your life, the camp needs her, the town needs her." Bobby pointed at Daisy. "Your mutt even needs her. I can't put it any plainer than that."

Bobby was right.

Dean had to talk to Priscilla, to apologize for being the biggest idiot in the world and, if it wasn't too late, tell her he loved her and wanted her to be in his life. He might not agree with her covering for her sister, but he understood all too well about loyalty, something he'd witnessed time and time again in the veterans he'd helped. They had each other's backs both on the battlefield and off. "Where do I start? Los Angeles is a bit bigger than Destiny."

Bobby grinned and pulled out his cell phone. "First, get yourself in the shower. The sooner you resemble a human being the better. Then pack a bag."

Dean stood up and started for his bedroom, then paused and turned back. "I'm not just going to show up on her doorstep, am I? Or at her office?"

"No, you'll need some help to do this right. I've still got some connections in L.A. Don't worry, she'll never know what hit her."

Stripping off his shirt, Dean hoped his friend was right as he headed for the shower, praying it wasn't too late for him to fix the biggest mistake of his life.

Chapter Fourteen

The mansion gleamed with candlelight as an orchestra played softly in the background. The crème de la crème of Beverly Hills were there, talking and dancing, the gentlemen clad in tuxedos and the ladies in long gowns. Priscilla's was a floor-length pink chiffon, the strapless bodice setting off her diamond jewelry to perfection, but she felt pale and lifeless, wishing she was back in her jeans, running around Camp Diamond with the kids.

With Dean.

She'd been home for three days and had yet to speak with her father, who was traveling again, but she and Jacqueline had talked on the phone a few times. Priscilla had been surprised to find Elizabeth, her father's secretary, waiting for her and Snake at the Beverly Hills house when she arrived on Tuesday morning with the news that her sister had voluntarily entered a treatment facility in New Mexico.

The news had been a shock, despite the alcohol she'd

smelled on her sister's breath the night of the auction. Priscilla was still coming to terms with all that her sister had done in the past month or so, but she was glad Jacqueline was finally getting the professional help she needed.

"Here, sugar, you look as if you need this." Lisa joined her at the far end of the crowded ballroom, two champagne glasses in her hands. "Have I told you yet how beautiful you look tonight?"

Priscilla smiled as she took the glass, even though she wasn't in the mood to drink. "Seeing that I am wearing one of your designs, you have to say that."

Lisa clicked the edge of her glass to Priscilla's and then raised it to her lips. "I don't know why you just don't call him."

Her friend's simple statement cut straight to her heart, but Priscilla pretended not to hear her as she looked out over the crowd, not really seeing any of them. No, what she saw were the people in a small ranching town who'd welcomed her into their lives with such friendliness, the amazing kids at the camp, the man she'd come to care for more deeply in a way she'd never felt before…

"It's no use." Priscilla looked down at the thousands of tiny bubbles shimmering in her champagne flute. "I already told you, he's made up his mind that Destiny and I, not to mention him and I, are as natural a fit as…well, as…"

"As a cowboy in Beverly Hills?"

At the familiar low tones, Priscilla looked up, her fingers tightening around the glass, that same burst of warmth springing to life deep inside her that always happened at the sight of the man making his way toward her.

Dean looked amazing in a black tuxedo and a dark Stetson, causing many in the ballroom to turn and watch him as he walked the few steps to her side. He kept his gaze locked on her. When he finally stood before her, she realized she was alone with him, her friend having mysteriously disappeared. He offered her a smile that was one part sexy and the rest charmingly nervous.

Stunned by his sudden appearance, Priscilla said the first thing that came to her mind. "I thought you didn't own a cowboy hat."

His smile was now the irresistible one she'd grown accustomed to during their time together in Destiny. "I wanted to make sure I stood out in your crowd."

Oh, he did that in ways he couldn't possibly imagine.

"Is there someplace where we can speak privately?"

His question was almost the same one, word for word, that she'd asked him a week ago after the auction. Uncertainty filled his eyes as she remained silent, but then Priscilla nodded and pointed toward the gardens visible through the wide-open French doors all along one side of the room.

"After you." He motioned for her to step in front of him. Priscilla did, her eyes fluttering closed for a moment when she felt the heat of his touch at her back as she walked out onto the enormous patio.

Pausing to leave her glass behind on the ornately carved stone wall that separated the patio from the well-manicured green lawn, she chose a private path hidden among defined boxwood hedges and flowering bushes dressed up for tonight's festivities with row after row of twinkling lights.

She finally stopped near a stone bench and turned to find Dean had removed his hat. "Not used to wearing that?" she asked.

"It was making it hard to see you and I've missed seeing you." His voice was low as his gaze roamed over her. "You are so beautiful, and if you don't mind me asking…"

His voice trailed off. She had no idea what he was going to say next.

"What kind of shoes are you wearing?"

Priscilla laughed, his silly question making her feel all bubbly inside, no champagne required. She lifted up the hem of her dress and pointed to her toes, showing off the high-heeled sandals that were nothing more than a few straps of light pink material decorated with rhinestones.

"Hmm, very nice, but I think I like you better in those work boots you wore at the camp."

His words set off a flutter in her heart. "So do I, actually. These beauties aren't as comfortable as they used to be."

A brightness filled Dean's eyes as he grinned and tugged at the collar of his shirt. "Me? I've never felt more out of place in my life."

"Well, you look amazing."

His smile softened. "Thanks."

"What are you doing here?" she finally asked. The small talk was driving her crazy and she was unable to hold back her curiosity any longer. "How did you know where to find me tonight?"

"Through Bobby and a few of his friends, one of them being your assistant, who is a big racing fan. I arrived in Los Angeles this morning and spent the rest of the day being buffed and shined and stuffed into this monkey suit, but it was all worth it because I needed to see you again. To talk to you."

Priscilla opened her mouth to speak, but Dean stopped her by gently pressing his finger to her lips.

"To tell you how sorry I am…for everything." He dropped his hand and placed his Stetson on the bench before turning back to her. "You must've seen that magazine I left in your room. Please believe me, I didn't say those things. Well, I didn't say them the way they reported it. You were great with the kids at the camp, and the ideas you came up with made it a better place for them. Not to mention how you got the whole town behind your auction."

Priscilla blinked hard. The tears were back again, but this time they were happy ones.

"And I was a complete jerk about your sister, too. I should've been more understanding. I'd do anything—okay, just about anything—for my brothers and sisters."

Priscilla reached out and took his hand, loving how his fingers instinctively laced with hers. "No, you were right. I was only trying to cover up a situation instead of facing it head-on. I don't know if you even care, but Jacqueline is getting help, professional help, and I'm so hoping that it works for her."

He gave her a gentle squeeze. "Of course I care."

"And I should've known better about that article. Lord knows I've had enough experience with the tabloids, but the timing of it all..."

Dean took a step closer and brought one hand to her cheek. "I know all about timing. When I woke up Tuesday morning and found out you had left town, I wanted to hop on the first plane that would get me here to you."

Priscilla swallowed against the hope that caused a lump to form in her throat. "Why?"

"You haven't guessed? I don't want to lose you." He lowered his brow until his forehead rested against hers, pressing a soft kiss to her temple. "I need you in my life, Priscilla. I know we haven't known each other for very long, but I fell in love with you the first time I saw you. I want to find a way to make this work, to make us work, even if it means my staying here.... If you feel the same way about me, that is."

Dean's words thrilled her and that tiny flutter expanded into a joyous elation. "What if I don't want to stay here?" she asked, trying to hold back her happiness and wishing he would ask her to return home with him.

He straightened, and his brows dipped in confusion.

"What about your job? I want you in Destiny full-time, as does Daisy, but if you need to be—"

"I need to be where you are!" Priscilla flew at him, loving how Dean enveloped her in his strong arms, the world melting away as he lifted her so her high heels weren't even touching the ground. "Beverly Hills doesn't feel like home anymore, not like being in Destiny."

His handsome face broke into a dazzling smile. "Are you sure that's what you want, princess?"

"I want you, Dean Zippenella. I love you and if Destiny is your home, it's going to be my—and Snake's—home, too."

He slowly lowered his mouth to hers and she met him halfway in a kiss that spoke of the passion and promise of a shared future, in a small town where fate had brought them together.

* * * * *

If you liked Dean and Priscilla's story,
Don't miss any of
USA TODAY *bestselling author*
Christyne Butler's
WELCOME TO DESTINY *series.*

THE COWBOY'S SECOND CHANCE
THE SHERIFF'S SECRET WIFE
A DADDY FOR JACOBY
WELCOME HOME, BOBBY WINSLOW
HAVING ADAM'S BABY
FLIRTING WITH DESTINY

Available from Harlequin Special Edition.

Enjoy this sneak preview of
DATING FOR TWO
by USA TODAY *bestselling author Marie Ferrarella!*

***

"Well, you'll be keeping your word to them—I'll be the one doing the cooking."

One of the things he'd picked up on during his brief venture into the dating realm was that most professional women had no time—or desire—to learn how to cook. He'd just naturally assumed that Erin was like the rest in that respect.

"Didn't you say that you were too busy trying to catch up on everything you'd missed out on doing because you were in the hospital?"

"Yes, and cooking was one of those things." She laughed. "A creative person has to have more than one outlet in order to feel fulfilled and on top of their game. Me, I come up with some of my best ideas cooking. Cooking relaxes me," she explained.

"Funny, it has just the opposite effect on me," he said.

"Your strengths obviously lie in other directions," she countered.

Steve had to admit he appreciated the way she tried to spare his ego.

He watched Erin as she practically whirled through his kitchen, getting unlikely ingredients out of his pantry and his cupboard. She assembled everything on the counter within easy reach, then really got busy as she began making dinner.

He had never been one who enjoyed being kept in the dark. "If you don't mind my asking, exactly what do you plan on making?"

"A frittata," she said cheerfully. Combining a total of eight eggs in a large bowl, she tossed in a dash of salt and pepper before going on to add two packages of the frozen mixed vegetables. She would have preferred to use fresh vegetables, but beggars couldn't afford to be choosers.

"A what?"

In another pan, she'd quickly diced up some of the ham she'd found as well as a few slices of cheddar cheese from the same lower bin drawer in the refrigerator.

She was about to repeat the word, then realized that it wasn't that Steve hadn't heard her—the problem was that he didn't know what she was referring to.

Opening the pantry again, she searched for a container of herbs or spices. There were none. She pushed on anyway, adding everything into the bowl with the eggs.

"Just think of it as an upgraded omelet. You have ham and bread," she said, pleased.

"That's because I also know how to make a sandwich without setting off the smoke alarm," he told her.

"There is hope for you yet," she declared with a laugh.

Watching her move around his kitchen as if she belonged there, he was beginning to think the same thing himself—but for a very different reason.

***

Don't miss DATING FOR TWO,
coming July 2014 from Harlequin® Special Edition.

HSEEXP0614

HARLEQUIN
A Romance FOR EVERY MOOD